The Blood-and-Thunder Adventure on
Hurricane Peak

OTHER YEARLING BOOKS YOU WILL ENJOY:

NONSTOP NONSENSE, *Margaret Mahy*
A FINE WHITE DUST, *Cynthia Rylant*
SOUP, *Robert Newton Peck*
SOUP AND ME, *Robert Newton Peck*
SOUP FOR PRESIDENT, *Robert Newton Peck*
SOUP ON FIRE, *Robert Newton Peck*
SOUP ON WHEELS, *Robert Newton Peck*
BEETLES, LIGHTLY TOASTED, *Phyllis Reynolds Naylor*
NIGHT CRY, *Phyllis Reynolds Naylor*
THE WITCH HERSELF, *Phyllis Reynolds Naylor*

YEARLING BOOKS/YOUNG YEARLINGS/YEARLING CLASSICS are designed especially to entertain and enlighten young people. Patricia Reilly Giff, consultant to this series, received her bachelor's degree from Marymount College and a master's degree in history from St. John's University. She holds a Professional Diploma in Reading and a Doctorate of Humane Letters from Hofstra University. She was a teacher and reading consultant for many years, and is the author of numerous books for young readers.

For a complete listing of all Yearling titles, write to
Dell Readers Service, P.O. Box 1045,
South Holland, IL 60473.

MARGARET MAHY

The Blood-and-Thunder Adventure on
Hurricane Peak

Illustrated by WENDY SMITH

A Yearling Book

Published by
Dell Publishing
a division of
Bantam Doubleday Dell Publishing Group, Inc.
666 Fifth Avenue
New York, New York 10103

ISBN: 0-440-40422-3

Reprinted by arrangement with Macmillan Publishing Company

Printed in the United States of America

March 1991

10 9 8 7 6 5 4 3 2 1

OPM

Many Happy Hurricanes
to Nicholas Simon

Contents

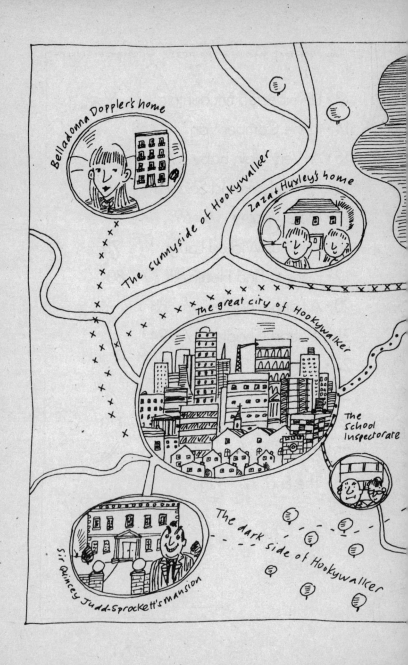

Belladonna Doppler's home

The sunnyside of Hookywalker

Zaza + Huxley's home

The great city of Hookywalker

The School Inspectorate

The dark side of Hookywalker

Sir Quincey Judd-Sprockett's mansion

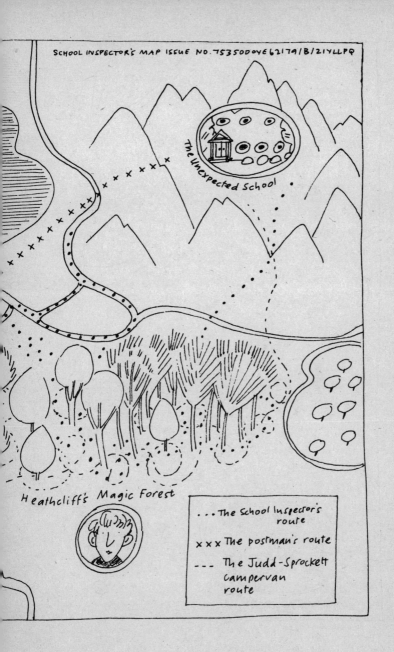

The Blood-and-Thunder Adventure on
Hurricane Peak

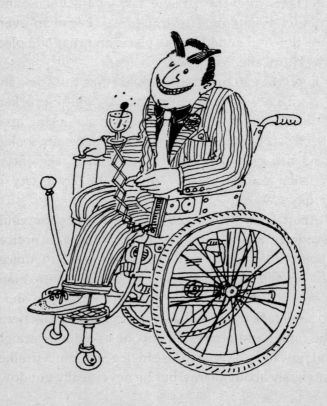

1 · A Very Wicked Industrialist

Most stories start in one place and then go in all directions, but the strange tale of the blood-and-thunder events on Hurricane Peak began in every direction and ended in one place, and that one place was Hurricane Peak itself.

Every blood-and-thunder story has a villain, and this villain's name was Sir Quincey Judd-Sprockett. He had beady little eyes and black hair sticking up in two twists over his temples, which made him look as if he had grown horns. He lived in a magnificent mansion on the shady side of the great city of Hookywalker.

Apart from his wickedness (which anyone could recognize at a glance) the other thing you noticed about him was that he had only one leg. Sir Quincey got around in a motorized wheelchair with many clever attachments such as a tiny computer and a cocktail cabinet, as well as a secret rocket launcher in the right-hand armrest. If anyone asked him straight out how he had come to lose his leg Sir Quincey talked carelessly about sharks, but he never really got down to details and, as he told lies whenever it suited him, no one could be sure just what had happened to it.

Just lately Judd-Sprockett products—wheelchairs, camper vans, computers, and so on—had been breaking down everywhere. People were up in arms about it; some even banged on the door of his mansion in the early hours of the morning demanding their money back.

"Slubberdegullion, Aunty, why is it my stuff never *works* properly?" cried Sir Quincey to his Aunt Perdita. "It's driving me bananas."

He hated when his wheelchair broke down, for he was afraid he might find himself banging on his own door and asking himself for his own money back. (That's what being driven bananas means.)

Sir Quincey's aunt was an adopted aunt, in fact, for he had no relations of his own, and he had agreed to pay her to be an aunt to him. All you could see of her, usually, were her feet sticking out from under the wheelchair. She was a wonderful motor mechanic as well as an excellent aunt, and spent a lot of time fixing up her adopted nephew's faulty technology for him.

"I've told you over and over again," she shouted

from under the wheelchair. "You're not a real inventor, only a villain. Stick to what you're good at."

Sir Quincey tried to give a wicked laugh, but he began coughing instead. Fortunately, he had a tape recording of a wicked laugh in the cassette player set in the left arm of his wheelchair and he quickly turned it on.

Har har har har har! went the wicked laugh for about five minutes. When it had finished, Sir Quincey pressed the rewind button and began to tell his aunt his wicked plans so that she would be able to jog his memory if he were to forget them. Actually, it was Aunt Perdita's memory that needed jogging, for she could remember only the last forty years. Anything that had happened to her before that was veiled in mystery.

"First, I want to start mining on Hurricane Peak," began Sir Quincey. "I know the Unexpected School is already on Hurricane Peak but I have plans to get rid of that institution. In fact I'd go up there and get rid of it with my rocket launcher, only it is spring in the next day or two and the pigweed will be in flower, and you know how one whiff of the flowering pigweed immediately gives me terrible hay fever. So I've been on the phone to the Education Department this morning, and they have promised me faithfully to send school inspectors up Hurricane Peak tomorrow. If they find one single thing wrong with the school— not enough pupils or not enough science and math— they will close the school down like *that*!" He clapped his hands together loudly, and then jumped in fright at the noise he had made.

"My second plan is to marry the beautiful inventor Belladonna Doppler," he went on. "I've already had her house burgled three times, but my burglars can never find any working drawings or blueprints, so I think she must keep the plans of all her inventions in her head. Aunty, I must have that head and all the inventions it contains, so I've decided to marry her."

"But suppose she does not want to marry you?" yelled his Aunt Perdita from under the wheelchair.

"She will, she will, when she gets my letter," Sir Quincey cried. "A pink letter with real gold ink! She'll be round here in a flash begging for my hand in marriage. And when we're married I will keep her busy inventing day and night. What with her doing the inventing, and no more Judd-Sprockett technology breaking down, and me marketing her inventions, I shall soon be a billionaire! No one will ask for their money back and I'll get a good night's sleep . . . apart from my guilty conscience and nightmares, that is."

But it is all very well for a villain to have wicked plans. They don't always work out. For instance, little did Sir Quincey know that, on that very day, the Unexpected School was to have a great piece of good luck—or rather, two pieces of good luck, and those two pieces of good luck were Huxley Hammond and his sister, Zaza.

2 · Huxley Hammond and His Sister, Zaza

On the sunny side of Hookywalker lived Huxley Hammond, a boy who liked to write bloodthirsty stories, and his sister, Zaza, who liked to draw the pictures to match. They had filled many notebooks with tales and drawings that made their parents go pale and wobbly at the knees.

"I'm sick of notebooks," said Huxley. "I want to go on to something bigger."

As it happened, it was the eleventh wedding anniversary of their dear parents. Since the Hammonds had just had all the bedrooms of their house painted a beautiful pure white, and as Mr. and Mrs. Hammond didn't care to celebrate a wedding anniversary in a house smelling strongly of paint, they went out and spent the evening eating lobster and drinking French champagne and dancing the twist, which had been popular in the days of their youth. However, when they came home they found that Huxley had written a thrilling blood-and-thunder story in small, neat printing from the very top of his newly painted bedroom wall to the very bottom of it.

"I couldn't help it," Huxley told them. "The wall looked like a huge white page. I just *had* to write a story on it."

But Huxley's parents were not writers and did not understand that a great, white, empty space just has to have something written on it.

"Oh, what a gruesome blood-and-thundery story," cried Mrs. Hammond, taking off her glasses and going wobbly at the knees. "Why don't you write something nice—about real life?"

But Mr. Hammond was particularly furious. "If you want blood-and-thunder, you shall have blood-and-thunder," he roared. "I am sending you to the Unexpected School on the top of Hurricane Peak."

"Oh, no," cried Mrs. Hammond. "That's going too far."

"Oh, yes," said Mr. Hammond. "The unexpected principal, Mrs. Desirée Thoroughgood, is a real tartar. That's what Huxley needs . . . a real tartar. *She'll* give him blood-and-thunder until he's sick of it!"

"What about me?" asked Huxley's sister, Zaza. She had blue eyes and golden hair, but she was even more blood-and-thundery than Huxley. "Huxley wrote the words but I drew the pictures."

Mr. and Mrs. Hammond went back into Huxley's room and had another look at the wall. Then they came back, looking very pale, and said that Zaza must be sent to the Unexpected School, too.

"Mrs. Desirée Thoroughgood will soon get rid of

your blood-and-thunder habits," they said. "It is for your own good."

"But I want to be a writer," cried Huxley. "I want to write creepy-crawly horror stories."

"And I want to draw covers for science-fiction books," cried Zaza.

"Nonsense," said their father, picking up the phone. "In your hearts you both want to be bank managers, or famous industrialists like Sir Quincey Judd-Sprockett (only not quite so wicked). You are too young to know what you really want. It is a parent's job to tell you."

He dialed the number of the Unexpected School on Hurricane Peak but, as usual, the line was down owing to the hurricane. They had to communicate with the school by radio telephone. There were a lot of clicks and bursts of static.

"Hello, this is the Unexpected School," said a strange, mewing voice. It sounded like a cat, but Mr. Hammond thought it was due to atmospheric disturbance.

"Am I speaking to Mrs. Desirée Thoroughgood?" he asked. "I have two children who need her special attention."

"Mrs. Thoroughgood is away at a conference," said the strange voice. "This is the head prefect speaking. I will connect you with the deputy principal, Mr. Warlock."

Mr. Hammond was disappointed at missing the chance of speaking to Mrs. Desirée Thoroughgood, but Mrs. Hammond told him not to worry.

"Mrs. Thoroughgood is always very busy," she said. "No one has spoken to her for years."

The deputy principal, Mr. Warlock, came to the radio telephone. He said the Unexpected School would be very happy to take Huxley and his sister, Zaza. "Thank goodness! That will bring the roll numbers up," Mr. Hammond heard him mutter to himself. He told Mr. and Mrs. Hammond to mark the children's names on all their clothes with indelible ink and to put them (along with the money for the first term's fees) on the helicopter that flew to Hurricane Peak every day to pick up the rubbish.

"It is the safest way to travel," the deputy principal told them. "You don't have to go over the wibbly-wobbly bridge or under the waterfalls, and the helicopter flies in while the hurricane is blowing around the back of the mountain."

"Tomorrow is Tuesday and I will put them on the helicopter then, without fail," said Mr. Hammond. "Tell Mrs. Thoroughgood that what they need is plenty of math and science."

Mr. Warlock was silent for a moment. Then he said that he would pass the message on.

The following day, Huxley and his sister, Zaza, together with their suitcases, were loaded onto the rubbish helicopter, which took off for the Unexpected School on Hurricane Peak in the Pigweed Mountains.

"I wonder if the Unexpected School is a little bit blood-and-thundery...even dangerous," said Huxley, "or if it is slow but safe, just like every other school in the world."

Of course, they did not know that what with Sir Quincey Judd-Sprockett threatening the school, it was about to become more unexpected than anyone, even Mrs. Desirée Thoroughgood, had ever intended.

3 · Belladonna Doppler and Her Cat, Tango

While Sir Quincey plotted and gloated, while Huxley and Zaza were being whirled up into the Pigweed Mountains in the rubbish helicopter, Belladonna Doppler opened the door of her laboratory and gasped with horror.

Belladonna Doppler was a ginger-haired inventor (beautiful, even though she did have sticking-out ears) who lived in a tall house on the very edge of the great city of Hookywalker.

Her laboratory had big windows with a beautiful view of Hookywalker and the Pigweed Mountains, which looked very blue and magical in the distance. On a good day she could even make out Hurricane Peak, with a shifting halo of cloud showing just where the hurricane was and how fast it was going. But this morning Belladonna was too cross to look at the view or to check the hurricane.

She had been anticipating a good day's inventing. (She was working on a singing bird bath, and a car horn that shouted *Look out! Look out, you idiot!* so that poor, confused drivers wouldn't have to shout it for themselves.) But burglars had been in for the third time that week and her whole laboratory had been turned upside down and left in a terrible mess. The burglars had opened cupboards, pulled drawers out, prized the carpet up, and cut the cushions open. They had even emptied out the jar where Belladonna kept her colored pencils as well as her pen that could write in black and red and green.

Sighing deeply, she fetched a rubbish bag and began to tidy up, complaining all the time to her companion. This was a handsome, black tomcat called Tango who did some dusting and light cooking and stopped mice from making nests in her inventions.

"When will they learn that there's nothing to steal from my house?" she complained. "I carry the plans for all my inventions in my head."

Of course, she did not know that, what with the ginger hair *on* it and wonderful inventions *in* it, her

12

head had attracted the attention of Sir Quincey Judd-Sprockett, who was planning to marry her. And she was so busy tidying up that she did not notice a Judd-Sprockett "Stickybeak" periscope for curious neighbors poking up over the balcony windowsill or realize she was being spied on. Even Tango did not notice this. He was too busy concentrating on his own plans. Cats are like that.

"It's not very restful with burglars coming in every day," he said, cunningly. "Why don't we go on holiday for a while?"

Belladonna stopped to consider, but while she was considering, there came a loud knock at the door.

"Ah," said Tango, looking pleased. "The postman! I wonder what *he's* got for us today?" And he ran eagerly to open the door, like a cat that expects something.

4 · The Unexpected School

The Unexpected School had been carved into the very top of Hurricane Peak. It was lashed by the hurricane six or seven times a day (for it took just over three hours for the hurricane to blow all the way round the peak and to come back to the beginning again).

When Huxley and Zaza Hammond climbed down the rope ladder out of the rubbish helicopter, the deputy principal was waiting to meet them. He was a tall young man wearing a swirling black cloak covered with magical words like *abracadabra* and *anaxagorillaballirogaxana*, a long word that can be spelt the same way forward and backward. His hair was bright ginger in color and very bushy, but this was a good thing, for though he was very handsome, his ears did stick out like jug handles and if his hair hadn't been so bushy and bright they would have seemed to stick out even more.

"I am Heathcliff Warlock," he said. "I suppose you can both see at a glance that I am a sorcerer. No use trying to hide it!"

Huxley and Zaza had already worked this out.

"We tend to specialize in magic at this school," Heathcliff went on casually, shuffling a pack of cards, while behind him the rubbish helicopter rapidly lowered its grabs to pick up the bags of school rubbish. "I know your father said you wanted plenty of science and math, and I promised I would pass the message on to Mrs. Thoroughgood. But, actually, Mrs. Thoroughgood has been away for quite a while, and I thought it might upset your father if I mentioned it. Of course, as soon as Mrs. Thoroughgood returns I *will* pass the message on, so I was telling the truth. And I have absolute faith that she will come back one day, indeed probably quite soon. Now, come inside and please hurry, because the hurricane is about to arrive."

As he spoke they could hear the hurricane whipping and whooping up behind them. The rubbish helicopter whirled away in panic.

"You told our father Mrs. Thoroughgood was away

at a conference," said Huxley, as they hurried up the school stairs.

"I always tell parents that," Heathcliff Warlock replied, tossing the cards into the air, where they disappeared. "I find it calms them, and it may even be true. I really hope it is. But the story of Mrs. Thoroughgood's absence is a troubling tale—even a little bit blood-and-thundery, I am sorry to say. I wonder if I should tell you. Yes, I think I should. It is best to be honest—well, as honest as possible."

He slammed the stone door in the face of the disappointed hurricane and went on talking as he rolled a big boulder against the door. As he led them to a room marked *Deputy Principal's Office*, he said, "You see, many years ago—well before I came to teach here—Mrs. Thoroughgood had a very troublesome pupil called Bottomley Quince. I won't go into all the details, but he bullied little children and made them invest their pocket money in a bank he had started himself, and then wouldn't let them take it out again but loaned it to older pupils at a high rate of interest. Naturally, when Mrs. Thoroughgood found out, she was furious. Bottomley Quince saw her coming after him, seized his wicked profits, and shot outside, with Mrs. Thoroughgood in close pursuit. Unfortunately, at that very moment the hurricane was at its height, and of course they were both blown away. In fact, they haven't been seen for forty years. However, forty years is nothing to a woman like Mrs. Thoroughgood, and I have faith that she'll be back any moment now."

Huxley and Zaza could see they had come to the right kind of school. Not only was it carved into the side of a mountain peak, but exciting things happened to people who attended it.

"I might write a story about that," cried Huxley.

"I might draw the pictures," said Zaza.

"Please do," said Heathcliff, taking an ace of hearts from Huxley's top pocket and staring at it in amazement. "But first, you must fill out these pink forms, invented by Mrs. Thoroughgood herself. Write down your names and your parents' names and their phone number and how much money they make, and things like that, and while you do that I'll look at the view."

As Huxley and Zaza filled out the forms the deputy principal wrapped himself in his cloak and stood at the window sighing to himself and flicking the ace of hearts through his fingers. Other cards came out of nowhere and soon he was shuffling the full pack again.

Outside, the hurricane raged by, sweeping a lot of things along with it ... leaves, sticks, mice, eagles, flocks of goats and so on, but you could make out the great city of Hookywalker on the plain below, all sparkling and magical in the distance.

"Ah, Belladonna!" Zaza heard him sigh. She wondered who Belladonna was. But, as it took Huxley and Zaza a long time to fill out the forms, I might as well take you back to Hookywalker to check on Belladonna and the knock on her door.

5 · A Pink Proposal

The postman, panting loudly, held his right hand over his heart in a dramatic fashion. He had just climbed two-hundred-and-seventy-two stairs and was making a great fuss over it.

"Oh, I see you've had the burglars in again," he wheezed, staring curiously past Tango at the disordered room.

"Never mind that!" said Tango impatiently. "Where's the mail?"

"Registered letter for Belladonna Doppler," the postman groaned. With his left hand he held out a large, pink letter. "You have to sign for it."

"The burglars have stolen my pens," Belladonna cried.

"I'll lend you mine," said the postman, leaping through the door, for he wanted to be there when Belladonna opened the pink letter. He was very interested in the letters he delivered, and hated not knowing exactly what was inside them. "My pen writes in red and black and green."

Belladonna turned the pink letter over, staring at it with great surprise.

"Shall I read it to you?" the postman suggested hopefully, but she shook her head.

"A pink letter?" she exclaimed. "A pink letter addressed in gold ink for me?"

"There's real gold in that ink, too," said the postman. "I popped into the Goldminer's Association office on the way here and had it tested for you. Real gold!"

"Really?" said Belladonna. "Did you know gold has seventy-nine protons in its nucleus and an atomic weight of, oh, more or less one hundred and ninety-six?"

The postman did not know this, but neither did he care.

"I'll *tell* you what is in that letter," he cried. "We postmen develop an instinct about things like that. It's a proposal of marriage, that's what it is."

Belladonna dropped the letter as if it were red hot.

"It's from Sir Quincey Judd-Sprockett, the famous

and wicked industrialist," the postman explained.

"How do you know?" Belladonna asked, amazed at the highly developed instincts of the postman.

"Because it has his name written on the back in more gold ink," the postman explained. "Are you going to accept him? He is struck down with passionate love for you."

Belladonna drew herself up to her full height. In spite of her sticking-out ears she looked astonishingly beautiful.

"Certainly not!" she said. "I am in the middle of very delicate experiments. I am pursuing the ultimate constituents of matter and I don't want them to get away."

The postman shook his head. They didn't teach such scientific language at the school for postmen.

"I think you're making a big mistake," he told her disapprovingly. "Sir Quincey Judd-Sprockett has a mansion in the shadiest part of town with a swimming pool in the garden."

"Why are you praising him?" asked Belladonna, suspiciously. "You don't work for him secretly, do you?"

"Me? *Me* work for *him*?" cried the postman. "Never! I am a postman and I come from a long line of postmen. My father was a postman and his father was a postman and *his* father was a postman and ... "

"I believe you," said Belladonna quickly, crumpling up the pink letter and tossing it into the trash can. "Let's forget it. I've too much work to do tidying up after the burglars and pursuing the ultimate constituents of matter to bother about Sir Quincey Judd-Sprockett."

"I do have another letter to deliver here," the postman said, looking rather wistfully at the pink envelope. "But it's not much of a letter," he added, holding it out scornfully. "Look—it's covered with grubby paw marks. It comes from Hurricane Peak!"

"Oh, miaow!" cried Tango eagerly, rubbing around the postman's legs.

"That will be for my cat," said Belladonna, holding the crumpled, dirty letter rather gingerly and opening it for Tango. "He has a penfriend."

Of course, not one of them had yet noticed that they were being spied on through a Judd-Sprockett "Stickybeak" periscope.

And meanwhile, miles away on top of Hurricane Peak, Huxley and Zaza had finished filling out their pink forms and were about to meet Tango's penfriend.

6 · Three Unexpected Things about the Unexpected School

Once the forms were filled out and filed away, Heathcliff led Huxley and Zaza out of the deputy principal's office into the school hall, which was very like a large cave, filled with stalactites and stalagmites and glowworms. Carved on either side of the hall in enormous letters was the school motto, *Always Expect the Unexpected*.

"We take our motto very seriously," said Heathcliff Warlock. "Mrs. Thoroughgood herself invented it. She had the school built up here so that, what with the hurricanes and everything, we would always remember it."

"She forgot about expecting the unexpected when she chased Bottomley Quince out into the hurricane," Huxley pointed out.

"Oh, we all have our absentminded moments," Heathcliff Warlock said, absentmindedly drawing a string of flags of every country in the world from his large left ear, as magicians often do. "Anyhow, we still try to live up to her ideals.... The first unexpected thing about the Unexpected School is that we don't teach any science and math. Of course, I don't tell parents that. It upsets them, and they take their children away and send them to some other school down in Hookywalker. That brings us to the second unexpected thing about the Unexpected School: there are only six pupils including you two. According to Hookywalker law, a school has to have at least six pupils so I often have to cut one of the pupils in half (which I can easily do, being a magician) and count him or her as two. And I also count the head prefect as a pupil, though I don't think inspectors would accept that. She didn't come to meet the rubbish helicopter because she was cleaning her whiskers, but here she is now."

"Miaow!" said the head prefect, running down the long stone corridor to meet them. To the surprise of Huxley and Zaza the head prefect was a beautiful, long-haired tortoiseshell cat. She had a pure white chest, white paws, and magnificent white whiskers. She was as clean and neat as a good prefect ought to be.

"I shall love this school," said Zaza, stroking the head prefect, who purred and rolled over, showing her stomach, which was covered with crimpish, curdly, curly cream-colored fur—much more attractive than the stomachs of most head prefects.

"Oh, we all love this school," agreed Heathcliff. "But it has been a great struggle keeping our numbers up."

He began pulling roses out of the air, talking as he did so.

"The third unexpected thing about the school is that we haven't had a visit from the school inspectors for years and years, and we're terrified of what will happen when they do get here. There are forces of darkness in Hookywalker which would like to close this school down, you know."

"Why?" asked Zaza, for it seemed to her to be the best school she had ever attended.

"Forces of darkness have no respect for unexpected education," explained the head prefect in a purring voice. "You see, a certain well-known wicked industrialist, Sir Quincey Judd-Sprockett, is hoping to get mining rights on Hurricane Peak, which is full of iron ore with traces of gold, titanium, and zinc."

"They wouldn't let him mine a mountain with a school on it, would they?" cried Zaza, but Heathcliff Warlock groaned.

"If ever the school inspectors do get past the hurricane and inspect us, they'll find we don't teach science and math, so they'll close us down immediately," he cried.

"Why don't you start teaching it?" asked Huxley.

"Me? Teach science?" cried Heathcliff. "Never! Magic is the thing! Magic is a natural part of nature. Science isn't."

He snapped the fingers of his right hand several times (for his left was holding a big bunch of roses) and little blue and scarlet birds came out at each snap and flew into cracks in the rocks, where they turned into wonderful gemstones.

"But here we are in the classroom," he said. "I'll leave Zanzibar to introduce you to the others. I must arrange these flowers."

"Zanzibar?" asked Huxley, looking around in surprise.

"Me!" purred the head prefect. "I am Zanzibar." She spoke perfect English but with a slight Spanish accent. "This way, please. And ask any questions you feel like asking. I love telling people about the Unexpected School, particularly anyone who is helping to save the school from school inspectors and Sir Quincey Judd-Sprockett."

But at that very moment Sir Quincey had actually forgotten about the Unexpected School. His wicked thoughts were focused on romance, and on Belladonna Doppler's ginger-haired head.

25

7 · More Villains

As Sir Quincey sat dreaming of being married to
Belladonna Doppler, a secret door in his study burst
open and into the room tumbled two figures, one
weighty and one weasely. They were carrying a Judd-
Sprockett "Stickybeak" periscope between them.

The weasely one was none other than Amadeus
Shoddy, and the weighty one was his brutal son,
Voltaire. Everyone in Hookywalker knew they were
villains, even though they tried to seem nice and
drove an ice-cream van that played *Girls and Boys Come
out to Play* on tuned bells. They worked for Sir Quincey
in their spare time, and had spent the last three nights
breaking into Belladonna Doppler's laboratory or
lying on the balcony and spying on her.

Amadeus was weedy and wore a large hearing aid
that whistled and howled like a banshee, while
Voltaire was large and lumbering with hair coming out
of his ears and nose (and a lot of other places, too).
Although he had been sent to a good school, he had
worn earplugs the whole time, refusing to learn
anything useful, and as a result his words occasionally

came out the wrong way round. But Voltaire didn't care. He *liked* confusing people. He wore a carpenter's apron full of false noses, Monopoly money, sleeping potions, South American passports, and other equipment used by villains.

"Ah, my faithful helpers," cried Sir Quincey, beaming at them.

"This will cost you plenty, you old codfish," groaned Amadeus. "I'm a senior citizen, and late nights will be the death of me."

Sir Quincey looked rather pleased.

"And I need a bit of senseless violence," growled Voltaire, looking around for something to break.

"Oh well, we'll come to that in good time," said Sir Quincey, nervously. "Tell me about Belladonna. Did she get my letter? A pink one with writing in gold ink? Was she overwhelmed?"

"Gink with pold ink?" said Voltaire, sneering. "She threw it in the crash tan. It was more litter than letter to Bolladenna Dippler."

Sir Quincey turned a terrible shade of purple.

"Threw it in the trash can?" he wailed. "But there was real gold in that ink."

"Real gold!" cried the Shoddys greedily. They would have run straight back to Belladonna's trash can to try and get the thrown-away letter with its valuable address but for Aunt Perdita, who was leaning against the secret door with her oil can held at the ready. Neither of them wanted her to squirt them with oil, something she occasionally liked to do.

"Very well," cried Sir Quincey. "Enough is enough! I have had her house burgled three times. I have proposed to her, I have been patient ... even tender, but now I shall strike, and I shall strike tonight. Belladonna Doppler must be kidnapped."

"You are going to bidnap Dolladenna Kippler?" cried Voltaire Shoddy, at last looking impressed.

"No, *you* are!" said Sir Quincey. "Tonight!"

"Me?" cried Voltaire. "Me do something so weevil? Never!"

"Not a chance," agreed Amadeus.

"My conscience wouldn't let me," sighed Voltaire.

"Nor mine," agreed Amadeus.

"Nit in a mollion years," swore Voltaire, trying to look noble.

"Never *ever!*" shouted Amadeus.

"Ever *never!*" Voltaire shouted, even more loudly.

Sir Quincey took out a bag of money and jingled it in the air. Instantly both Shoddys fell on the ground before him and began polishing his single boot with kisses. Aunt Perdita contemptuously squirted oil across their backs.

"The mere sound of money, and there they are, fawning on you," she said scornfully.

"At the mere sound of money I could fawn on myself *and* lick my own boots," Sir Quincey declared, jingling the bag in his own earhole.

"Your own boot!" corrected Aunt Perdita. "You only have one."

Sir Quincey hated to be reminded he only had one of anything, "Okay," he cried, kicking the Shoddys away. "That's enough fawning. Get on with the kidnapping. Set off at twenty-two-hundred hours, and my dear adopted aunt and I will come and watch you."

"At twenty-two o'clock we will flong Billodenna Dappler, screaming for mercy, at your very foot," promised Voltaire, his hand on his heart.

"And then, " said Amadeus, "we'll help you throw the kids out of the Unexpected School. I *am* looking forward to that."

8 · An Unexpected Classroom

At first glance the classroom was not particularly unexpected. It was certainly untidy. There were four desks and each one had a pack of cards, a wand, and a top hat on it. There were colored streamers, balloons of all colors, a few white rabbits, and many bowls of goldfish. But it had the usual blackboard and the usual chalk. The windows were like deep portholes, and in front of each window was a life-size cardboard cut-out of an Unexpected pupil to deceive any inspectors skulking around outside who might be checking on the number of children in the school.

At the back of the classroom stood a large clock with human hands, and a particularly grand statue of Mrs. Desirée Thoroughgood, looking both good and thorough. It was carved out of the wood of the corkwood tree and was hung all over with raincoats. Huxley and Zaza admired the statue, but they were rather puzzled by a long line of stone boots just inside the door.

The classroom was not empty. Two children were catching up on a bit of homework. A fair-haired boy was encased in a block of wood on wheels, while a lively girl with a long braid was busy sawing him in half.

"Haven't you finished your homework yet, Joanna?" asked Zanzibar, lashing her tail sternly.

"Not the magic!" said Joanna. "I've done all the cooking and geography and I've written three poems. Of course, there's no math or science."

Zanzibar hissed, lashed her tail hard, and even flattened her ears. She hated to be reminded of the school's shortcomings.

"Anyhow, it's my turn to be sawn in half," the boy explained, his feet wriggling wildly, for being sawn in half tickles if it is properly done.

"But we have two new pupils," Zanzibar said. "We have a roll of six now. Maurice can stay in one piece."

"I can't stop halfway!" said Joanna, and suddenly Maurice was in two pieces, though his toes were still wriggling and his head was still giggling. Joanna spun the two pieces round to show there was no deception.

"Not too bad!" said Zanzibar. "Now put him together again. It's nearly time for school to begin."

"It is not!" muttered the clock.

"It is!" said Zanzibar. "I saw you sneaking back ten minutes."

"All right, then—I'll chime!" threatened the clock, and he did chime once very loudly and reproachfully, so that two other children, rushing into the room thinking it was time for a class, had to be introduced to Huxley and Zaza. These Unexpected pupils were called Leo and Mary. Leo was only seven, but he cooked most of the meals, for he was a talented chef. Mary wanted to be a vet and felt very lucky to be going to school where she had a wonderful chance of learning about a cat's point of view on good health. They both loved the Unexpected School dearly, and were pleased to find it had two new pupils.

"Zanzibar," cried Joanna in a worried voice, when the introductions were over. "I can't get Maurice together again. I've forgotten the right spell."

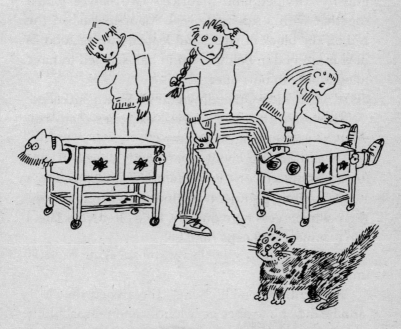

"Think hard!" cried Maurice, who did not want to spend a lot of time cut into two pieces. But though Joanna frowned and looked into the air, she could not remember the joining spell. None of the others was up to cutting people in half yet and, of course, Huxley and Zaza hadn't done even the smallest bit of magic. They were all relieved when Heathcliff Warlock swept into the room swirling his cloak very grandly.

"Oh, Joanna," he said crossly, when he saw Maurice was in two halves and Joanna had confessed that she had forgotten the spell. "You won't always have me around to tidy up after you." Then he waved his cloak and made a few mystic signs. There was a fanfare of ghostly trumpets and Maurice's two halves joined together with a satisfying *click*. Maurice pushed the top off the block of wood and leaped out, as good as new if not better. Being sawn in half seemed to have filled him with new energy.

"All right, kids! Quiet down now!" Heathcliff called. "We'll start with a few magical exercises. Zanzibar, why are you looking so dreamy?"

"I was thinking about tomorrow," Zanzibar confessed, confused for the moment. "I am expecting a letter from my penfriend in Hookywalker. I do hope the postman gets here quickly. He's often very late. I can't think what keeps him."

9 · An Idea for a Disguise

"If I call in the police," cried Belladonna Doppler, "the whole house will be filled with detective inspectors measuring things and taking fingerprints and I won't be able to concentrate. What shall I do?"

The postman had no idea. "I'd better be getting on now," he said quickly. "Hey ho, never a dull moment."

"Wait a moment," miaowed Tango. "I'll just dash off a note to my penfriend, Zanzibar." He ran to a drawer and pulled out a sheet of notepaper. "I can't wait to tell her all about the burglars."

Belladonna dropped a torn cushion into her trash bag and sighed.

"It's at moments like these that I miss Cousin Heathcliff," she said.

"Who?" asked the postman keenly, thinking he had heard a familiar name.

"Cousin Heathcliff," repeated Belladonna, staring down into the trash bag as if into a fortune-teller's glass. "He was a second cousin twice removed and I was very fond of him. He had the same fluffy ginger hair as I have, and the same sticking-out ears. He was very handsome as well as generous, clever, and kind-hearted. He could also tap-dance and play the banjo. But those talents were not enough!"

"Aren't they?" said the postman, surprised. "They would be enough for most people."

"Heathcliff was quite impossible," said Belladonna sternly. "You see, he was totally devoted to magic, and I am interested only in science. Magic!" Belladonna drew herself up scornfully. "I know that with a bit of magic we could tidy up this room in double-quick time, but it's against nature, and nature deserves respect. We scientists respect nature. We don't go around tricking it. Heathcliff and I quarreled. He strode off into the sunset and I haven't seen him since."

There was rather a sad pause after this.

"Isn't that funny!" said the postman. But he wasn't laughing. He was leaning in the doorway looking melancholy. "I know just how you must feel. I once loved the principal of the Unexpected School, Mrs. Desirée Thoroughgood, but I can't go into all that now. I'm already late with my rounds. I shouldn't have spent all this time here, but I get so interested in things I just can't tear myself away."

Meanwhile, Tango, after rubbing his paws in the fireplace until they were black, was dashing backward and forward across the paper, leaving a pattern of pad marks.

"Well," said the postman, very impressed, "I've heard of dashing off a note, but I've never seen anyone actually doing it before. There's no end to the fascination of the postal service." He took Tango's letter gingerly and put it in a special pocket of his postman's bag. "Well, see you tomorrow!"

He shut the door after him, but Belladonna did not turn around.

"I'm not sure I will be here," she said to Tango. "You are quite right. If burglars are going to break into my house, day after day, I might just as well go on holiday until they've gotten over it. I can do my inventing anywhere I like because I carry all my ideas in my head, and I take that with me wherever I go."

Tango leaped up. "By a curious coincidence," he cried, "I have just received an invitation to go and stay with my penfriend up on Hurricane Peak. Why don't we go together? I know a school isn't the usual place for a holiday, but there aren't many children there at present because they don't teach science and math, and . . ."

"What?" Belladonna exclaimed, interrupting him. "No math? No science? How will those children ever learn to invent anything? Tango, you're right! We must go to this school at once, and I will have a word with the teachers. But we'd better travel after dark, and we'd better go in disguise. I don't want burglars following me, and I don't want Sir Quincey Judd-Sprockett sending me more pink envelopes. This must be a real holiday."

"What shall we go disguised as?" asked Tango.

"You can go disguised as yourself," said Belladonna, "for people will probably think you are an entirely different black tomcat from the one you really are, but I will have to think carefully. I must take my cloak in case it turns cold and my overnight inventor's pack. But I need something to slip on over everything else so that I can put anyone who follows me off the track."

As she spoke she looked down at the rubbish bag in her hands and an amazing idea came into her head. Belladonna had that sort of head. No wonder Sir Quincey Judd-Sprockett was keen to gain power over it!

10 · A Reassuring Letter

That night, after a refreshing day of learning magic and writing a little poetry, Huxley wrote a reassuring letter to his father and mother.

Dear parents,
We arrived safely at the Unexpected School, and began work almost at once. I am afraid Mrs. Thoroughgood is dreadfully strict. We began with three hours of science and mathematics without resting once.

There are forty-two children here—that is, seven times six—and we all have to work very hard. Mrs. Thoroughgood says it is good for our characters to struggle, and I think she is right. The head prefect keeps us all in order, and the hurricane

storms past every three and a half hours. I began writing a
blood-and-thunder story but Mrs. Thoroughgood took away
my pen that writes in three colors.

I can feel the school is doing me a lot of good already.

Your loving son, Huxley

He put the letter in an envelope and addressed it
carefully. Then he took out a new blue notebook,
which Zanzibar had found for him, to write a story.
But his head was too full of cat prefects, magic, and
wicked industrialists, and for the first time in years
not a single blood-and-thunder idea occurred to him.
Quite quickly he gave up and went to sleep.

11 · Going on Holiday

The Hookywalker Police Department happened to be having an economy drive, and Police Constable Davenport Davis and his twin sister, Police Constable Dreadnaught Davis, had had their police car taken away from them. They were issued flashlights and roller skates instead. However, this suited them very well, for they were fond of skating and had come in second in the Hookywalker Pairs Championship.

Skating as one Davis, they glided gracefully through the midnight streets, first on their right legs, then on their left, bravely flashing their torches into all sorts of dark corners. Cats and rats hid in holes at the approach of the police, but one particular black tomcat took no notice at all. Tango (for it was he) had a clear conscience and, sitting on top of a trash can, he looked sharply around while pretending to wash himself.

The two police skated past. Tango, making sure they were out of sight, beckoned with his tail and at once a large trash bag bounded into view.

But the sudden rumble of skates behind them

41

meant the Davises were returning yet again.

Down shrank the trash bag, and torchlight passed harmlessly over it as the Davises skated by. When they were gone the trash bag rose, bouncing on its way once more.

But there was another sudden sound...this time of tinkling fairy bells. The trash bag crouched down again.

Girls and boys come out and play, intoned the bells invitingly. A pink ice-cream van, driven by pedal power, skidded round the corner, pedalled by two men, one weasely, one weighty.

Directly behind the ice-cream van came a wheelchair in which reclined a certain wicked industrialist (you can probably guess which one) wrapped in a fur coat, his adopted aunt clinging to the back of the chair. They were just about to go right past the trash bag when they saw the Davis twins skating gracefully

toward them on their way down the street.

"Evening, sir," the police constables said as one Davis, looking suspiciously at the ice-cream van. "What's going on here?"

"Oh, Officer," whined Amadeus, "we're just two nice clean crooks with a few innocent vices ..."

"We're not!" yelled Voltaire, "we're ice-cream cooks giving out new chiclate chop ices."

"That's right," Amadeus agreed eagerly. "Well, not *giving* exactly. More like *selling*!"

"I don't suppose you've noticed such a thing as a ginger-headed inventor wandering around the streets?" Voltaire asked them, speaking very clearly for once, as he wanted to make a good impression. "We all went round tonight to call on Dillabenna Dappler but she had just slipped out for a moment. Have you, by any chance, noticed her getting around this part of town?"

The Davises shook their heads. They hadn't seen anything so interesting.

"Now, that man over there is a famous, wicked undistrialist," explained Voltaire, jerking his thumb at Sir Quincey. "He's very anxious to get in touch with her if he can."

The Davises frowned. Being members of the police force, they naturally wanted to help a famous industrialist who was wicked as well, but they had not seen any ginger-headed scientists in that part of town. Then Davenport had a sudden idea.

"That trash bag!" he exclaimed. "We went skating by a moment ago and there was no trash bag, and yet when we came back..."

"I do believe you're right, Davenport," said Dreadnaught. "When we came skating back there was a brand new trash bag lying down.... Oh, it's gone!"

"That's strange," said Amadeus, who had turned his hearing aid on full and was listening intently. "I saw that trash bag.... It was edging off into the shadows, and I thought, 'Hello! Someone must have fallen into their own trash bag by accident. Either that or they've put the cat in it.' And I had a bit of a laugh to myself. But there it was—and *there it goes!*" he suddenly screamed. He pointed his ice-cream scoop like a gun at the trash bag, which had mysteriously put out legs and was running off into the blackest shadows of Hookywalker.

Over in the shadows Sir Quincey was so excited that he accidentally leaned on the left-hand button that started the cassette recording of the villainous laugh. As for Voltaire, he raced furiously after the trash bag, and might have caught it too, but for a black tomcat leaping between his scrambling feet, causing him to fall heavily to the ground. The two Davises fell over him, and Amadeus, pedaling madly, drove the ice-cream van (which fortunately was not very heavy) right over the lot of them. He then reversed into Sir Quincey's wheelchair, which was unable to dodge, for this Judd-Sprockett invention had seized up entirely. If it hadn't been for this, Belladonna might have been caught, in spite of her good disguise.

As it was, the bag escaped, accompanied by a black tomcat, leaving terrible confusion behind. The pair of them ran madly in the direction of Hurricane Peak, which was just visible in the distance, gleaming eerily in the flashes of lightning that constantly played around it.

"This is a funny way to begin a holiday!" Belladonna called out of the trash bag.

"Forward, Belladonna! Do not despair!" Tango reassured her. "Soon we'll be on Hurricane Peak and everything will be silent and serene (apart from the hurricane, of course). Keep right on to the end of the road! *Nil desperandum*, Belladonna! Forward! Advance!"

Fat chance! cried the Hookywalker echo, mockingly bouncing back from the walls and windows of the city.

12 · Rubbish from the Sky

How lovely for a boy longing to write blood-and-thunder mysteries to be woken by a roll of thunder on his very first morning in the Unexpected School! Huxley immediately wrote a second letter to his mother and father.

Dear parents, (he wrote)
I am working hard and I am already top of the class. I have put blood-and-thunder behind me. Mrs. Thoroughgood is very stern but fair. Could you send me some money and food urgently?
    Your loving son, Huxley.

Huxley knew just the sort of letter parents like to get. His letter may not have been strictly true, but he wanted them to be happy.

It is true in a poetical way, he thought, feeling like a real writer.

"Where shall I post my letters to my parents?" Huxley asked, returning to the classroom where the other children were already gathered. They were all watching Zaza draw science-fiction pictures of the fiercest kind.

"Wait until the postman comes," purred Zanzibar. "You won't have long to wait. In fact I think I hear him now." As she spoke, the tintinnabulation of a great, brass gong shook the whole school. Zanzibar fluffed out her tail.

"Ah," she murmured in a mysterious, purring voice. "Another letter from my penfriend in the city."

She ran to open the door, looking smug as she did so. The children watched her rather sadly, a little jealous of a cat who was not only a prefect but had a penfriend as well.

The postman came staggering in under the weight of his mail bag. He had only two letters to deliver that

day, but naturally he had to fill his bag with stones or he would have been blown right off the mountain.

"I'm worn out with climbing and crossing the wibbly-wobbly bridge and being soaked by the waterfalls," he lamented.

Distant footsteps were heard in the school corridor.

"He's coming, he's coming," hissed Maurice.

Heathcliff Warlock swept into the room, swishing his cloak, splendid in black clothes that made his fuzzy, ginger hair look particularly fuzzy and ginger, and his sticking-out ears seem somehow very heroic.

"School's in!" he shouted. "Get to your desks and take out your wands. Take off that postman's hat and get to work."

"Hold on a minute," cried the postman. "I'm not one of your Unexpected pupils. I'm the postman and I have a letter for you, Mr. Warlock!"

"Miaow!" cried Zanzibar.

"And for you, too," added the postman quickly. "It's a hard life," he added pathetically, "when I've got to climb up Hurricane Peak to deliver letters for cats, but the mail must get through, and the post office is too proud to use the rubbish helicopter."

Heathcliff seized his letter nervously.

"Perhaps...at last...can it be? A letter from Mrs. Thoroughgood? Or even...who knows...after all this time...Belladonna!" He blushed deeply, studying a huge letter covered with red sealing wax.

"Oh, dear," he muttered. "Is it another letter from Sir Quincey Judd-Sprockett demanding mining rights under the school? Oh, no. Even worse! It's from the Department of Education."

Meanwhile, the postman gave Zanzibar a letter covered with black paw prints.

"Ah," she sighed. "My penfriend has dashed off a note to me." And she carried it away to read it under a nearby desk.

As for Heathcliff, he read his letter three times, backward, sideways, and the right way up, but whichever way he read it, it made the same sort of sense just like *anaxagorillaballirogaxana*. He sighed very deeply.

"Children!" he cried. "Something has come up."

"Seeing where you live it couldn't very well go down, could it?" cried the postman, who was lingering, hoping to find out what was in the letter covered with red sealing wax. He pranced about laughing at his own joke, but no one else joined in. They all stood staring anxiously at Heathcliff.

"I knew it would happen some day," said Heathcliff, "and it's happening today! The inspectors are coming."

"I told you so," mewed Zanzibar, running out from under Huxley's desk. "What *will* they say when they find you are teaching magic instead of math and science?"

"I don't know," said Heathcliff gloomily. He sighed and ran his hands through his ginger hair. "It's at moments like these that I wish I had not quarreled with Belladonna."

"Belladonna?" asked Joanna curiously.

"Belladonna?" cried all the other children.

Heathcliff paced up and down the classroom. "A second cousin twice removed," he said at last. "Quite impossible, but there's no doubt she was very good at science and math. Oh, I loved her wildly—passionately—but we belonged to two different worlds."

The children, Zanzibar, and the postman listened intently to this romantic tale.

"We quarreled," Heathcliff said, "and I took on the job as matron at the Unexpected School. Hookywalker was too full of sad memories for me. Once I was here and found Mrs. Thoroughgood was missing I made myself deputy principal, and of course since then I have been too busy running the school to think much about Belladonna. And yet, you know, the odd thing was," he said, still pacing around the room, "Belladonna and I had a lot in common. We both wanted to change the world. We both wanted a bit of flash and glitter. But I wanted abracadabra, and she wanted quantum mechanics."

"Where's Belladonna now?" asked Leo, for the children were very curious about Heathcliff's private life. It was hard to imagine anyone falling in love with a teacher—even a teacher of magic.

"I don't know!" said Heathcliff. "I almost wish she were here. She was brilliant at science and math. She could make two times two equal any number you like to mention. That's known as calculus," he added proudly.

"It's funny your saying all this," said the postman in a wistful voice. "Did I ever mention that I once loved Mrs. Thoroughgood...still do, no matter where she's got to...and I think she fancied me. She used to give me some very significant looks when I delivered the mail in the morning. I was a young postman then of course, and I was rather shy, but just as I was plucking

51

up my courage to ask her out to the post office beanfeast, she was blown away in the hurricane and I haven't seen her for forty years. You know, with her at my side I might have risen to be postmaster general. But as it is I've stayed a simple postman."

Heathcliff looked sympathetically at the postman, and Huxley began taking a few notes, as many authors do when they hear a tale of sorrow. At that moment, though, the air began to throb powerfully and the children rushed to the window.

"It's the rubbish helicopter," cried Leo.

They clustered at the window, staring intently, for the rubbish helicopter was a magnificent sight, its rotors flashing as the grabs came down to collect the schools' rubbish bags that had been put out that morning.

"Hey!" cried Zaza suddenly. "It's not just collecting rubbish. It's actually dropping some off."

"They didn't tell me rubbish was being swapped around," cried Heathcliff, who had been gloomily re-reading the letter from the Department of Education and was not really interested in the rubbish collection. Now, however, hearing that rubbish was being lowered as well as lifted, he ran to the window. "Let me see! Oh, horrakapotchin! We'll have to bring that trash bag inside at once or rubbish will blow all over Hurricane Peak in the next hurricane."

"Let Zaza and me go," suggested Huxley. He had been longing for a chance to get out in the hurricane wearing those stone boots with which the children of the Unexpected School had all been supplied after Mrs. Thoroughgood and Bottomley Quince were blown away. The others were only too glad to let them have a turn, for the stone boots were very clumsy. So Huxley and Zaza slipped on a pair each, and thumped out as lightly as possible. Wearing stone boots made them feel like old established, well-accepted pupils of the Unexpected School.

Already the hurricane was making itself felt. It howled savagely as the main door was opened, roaring down the hall into the classroom, where it sent papers, silk handkerchiefs, flags, top hats, and chalk spiraling into the air. It took the combined strength of all the children as well as Heathcliff, Zanzibar, and the postman to hold the door shut while Huxley and Zaza, waving to the rubbish helicopter, clumped across the school yard and began dragging the strange rubbish bag back toward the classroom.

"Now!" cried Heathcliff. "Everyone ready? Open the door, let them in, then all slam it shut together."

"Open UP!" shouted Huxley and Zaza. The door was opened, and the roar of the hideous gale blasted past them into the classroom, where loose pages were once more whirled aloft and pens shot through the air like darts.

In rushed a handsome black tomcat while Huxley and Zaza successfully dragged the rubbish bag over the threshold.

"Everyone push!" yelled Heathcliff, and they all pushed hard till the door slammed shut. Quickly they rolled the boulder back behind it. The angry roar of the hurricane died away almost to nothing and they retreated down the hall.

"That's funny," said the postman, staring at the black cat. "Haven't I seen you somewhere before?"

But Tango (for it was he) had no time to listen to a mere postman. He had seen Zanzibar, his penfriend, and she had seen him.

"Miaow!" cried Tango.

"Miaow!" Zanzibar replied softly.

"Oh, miaow!" Tango exclaimed, staring at her intently.

"Ah, miaow!" Zanzibar answered, smiling.

"Miaow?" asked Tango quickly, impressed with her quick wit.

"Miaow!" Zanzibar responded, flicking the white tip of her tortoiseshell tail.

Naturally, everyone was very interested in this, particularly the postman; but before the children and Heathcliff could become further involved in the cut and thrust of cat conversation, something else began happening, something so unexpected that even the pupils and deputy principal of the Unexpected School were taken by surprise. The trash bag began to mumble and stretch itself. Then it put out a pair of legs at the bottom and a pair of arms at the side. It was obvious that someone was struggling to get out of it.

13 · Unexpected Encounters

"I seem to know those legs," the postman cried, staring at what was sticking out of the bottom of the rubbish bag.

Heathcliff Warlock seized the hand on the end of the arm which stuck out from its side.

"What a pretty hand!" he exclaimed. "And what is this? A ring with the crest of the Warlock-Doppler family. How does a rubbish bag come to be wearing a family ring?"

But at that moment the rubbish bag tore apart and Belladonna Doppler herself stepped out, her ginger hair looking particularly gingerish. She was carrying her little inventor's pack and wearing her black scientist's cloak, and though it was very crushed it was just possible to make out the mystic equations embroidered on it: $E = MC^2$ and so on.

"Heathcliff!" she cried.

"Belladonna!" Heathcliff cried back.

"Zanzibar!" exclaimed Tango.

"Tango!" Zanzibar mewed.

The children were fascinated. Even the Unexpected

School was seldom as unexpected as this.

The postman nodded like someone who recognizes an old friend.

"Well, I must get on with delivering letters," he said to the children. "Hurricanes, helicopters, family reunions...it's all in a day's work to a postman. They can sort it out for themselves," he added, apparently addressing the clock.

"Are we here? Have we arrived safely?" asked Belladonna, looking around the Unexpected School classroom with surprise.

"Yes, yes," cried the children.

However, life is dangerous even when it seems at its safest, and little did any of them know that, out on Hurricane Peak, villains and enemies were already at work.

14 · In the Camper Van

Not far from the school, in a hollow in the side of Hurricane Peak, a Judd-Sprockett camper van was parked, anchored with the Judd-Sprockett superanchor, an anchor usually used only by battleships and ocean-going liners.

The hurricane was dying down, and, there in a relatively calm spot, Sir Quincey and his Aunt Perdita watched as Voltaire pinned baby's diapers onto his wrinkled father, Amadeus.

"It's hard for a man of my age having to wear diapers," moaned Amadeus.

"They *suit* you, Diddykans," said Voltaire in a sinister tone of voice. He could remember that when he was a baby Amadeus had pinned diapers onto him, and had not always been careful with the pin, either. So he was pleased to be getting his own back.

"Yes, they look very nice," said Sir Quincey. "But who ever heard of a baby wearing a hearing aid and glasses. Take them off! He can do without them if he tries."

Amadeus and the hearing aid both emitted a howl of protest.

"Give the hearing aid to me!" cried Aunt Perdita. "I'll turn it into a two-way radio and then, when they take him in, he'll be able to report back to us." (A good aunt can be a blessing to a wicked industrialist.)

While Amadeus whined and complained and Perdita fiddled with the hearing aid, Sir Quincey drew Voltaire to one side.

"He isn't what I'd call a pretty baby," he grumbled. "I wouldn't adopt him if he were left on my doorstep. Can't we make him look a bit more—you know—*appealing*?"

"He's a baby, isn't he?" cried Voltaire. "They're bound to take him in, and once he's in there..." He nudged Sir Quincey, who hastily pressed the button of the cassette player on his wheelchair and the sound of wicked laughter was heard on Hurricane Peak.

"All right. Pop him into the baby carriage!" said Sir Quincey. "We'll have a go."

"It'll cost extra, me having to push this baby carriage in hurricane country," Voltaire warned as he set off, while Sir Quincey and his Aunt Perdita struggled back inside the Judd-Sprockett camper van, to monitor progress through the Judd-Sprockett control panel with which this particular camper van was equipped.

Seeing the hurricane storm past had made Aunt Perdita strangely thoughtful.

"Should I be helping Quincey with his wicked schemes, even if he is my adopted nephew?" she was asking herself. "There is something familiar about this place, but I can't quite . . ." The thunder growled and Aunt Perdita almost remembered whatever it was that she kept on almost remembering. However, in the end she gave up and focused her attention on the vital control panel.

15 · A Very Plain Baby

In the Unexpected School a great reunion was under way. Belladonna was telling everyone about her adventures on the way to the school. Huxley was taking notes, and Zaza was doing a few rough sketches. It had not been an easy journey.

"And then we crossed the wibbly-wobbly bridge." ("... wibble-wobble, wibble-wobble ..." Tango put in.) "But we took no notice. Of course, the Shoddys couldn't get their ice-cream van over it. They had to go back. We went up the ladders," Belladonna went on, hanging her cloak on the statue of Mrs. Thoroughgood, "before finding our way back onto the track. But suddenly we discovered we were being chased by the Judd-Sprockett camper van. They must have found another way up. It has optional tractor treads."

"You should have vanished," said Heathcliff, giving Belladonna a challenging look.

"I can't do vanishing," replied Belladonna regretfully. "I'm just working on intermolecular penetration now."

"*I* can vanish!" declared Heathcliff (and I am sorry to say he looked rather smug).

"Yes, but not without a magical cabinet!" said Belladonna sharply. "Anyhow, just as I was becoming tired, the rubbish helicopter came zooming overhead . . ."

Tango butted in. ". . . and we hitched a ride . . ."

". . . and here we are," finished Belladonna. "We arrived at the very place we were setting out for. Oh, Heathcliff! It *is* so nice to see you again. Imagine you being a teacher. It's very unexpected."

"Well, this is the Unexpected School," Heathcliff said. "It gives me a good chance to teach a bit of magic."

"I heard you didn't teach science and math," said Belladonna rather sternly, "but you do, don't you?"

There was an awkward pause. The clock cleared its throat. "Ten o'clock in the morning," it announced.

But just then the door gong was banged loudly and those who listened could make out, over the sound of the fading hurricane, the sound of big feet running away in the opposite direction.

Heathcliff turned pale.

"It can't be school inspectors, can it?"

"Those feet knocked at the door, then ran away again," said Mary comfortingly. "School inspectors are supposed to be brave."

"Open the door, then!" cried Heathcliff magnificently.

It was the work of a moment for Leo and Mary to put on their stone boots, roll away the boulder, open the door, and pull a battered-looking baby carriage into the room. Heathcliff, Belladonna and all the children peered into it. The cats stood on their hind legs and looked in too.

"Another Unexpected pupil," said Zanzibar. "Our numbers are creeping up."

But she sounded rather doubtful.

16 · A Hard-hearted Scientist

Heathcliff, Belladonna, the children, the postman, and the cats continued to look at the baby in dismay. It was very wrinkled, even for a baby; it was also badly in need of a shave, and whatever it had in its baby's bottle looked suspiciously like beer—which everyone knows isn't good for babies.

"Look at its hearing aid," said Joanna, astonished.

"This baby reminds me of someone," said Belladonna. "Someone I don't like. Tango! Can it be a relation of the wretched Shoddy brothers!"

Heathcliff read the note that was pinned to the baby.

"Oh, what a pathetic story!" he said. "This baby's father has to pay so much income tax that he can't afford to keep his seventeen little ones so he has had to give some of them away."

"I'm not surprised he gave this one away," said Belladonna in a suspicious voice. "May I see that note? As I thought! This writing is exactly like the writing of Sir Quincey Judd-Sprockett."

"How do *you* know?" asked Heathcliff suspiciously.

He had had many letters himself from Sir Quincey over the possibility of mining under the school, but they had all been typed, not hand-written.

"Only yesterday he sent a letter proposing to me," Belladonna explained.

Heathcliff turned slightly green. "So!" he cried angrily. "A simple magician isn't good enough for you. You have to be proposed to by a millionaire with a lot of unreliable technology at his disposal!"

Even the children could see that he was being worked on by unreasonable jealousy, a terrible complaint.

"Look at this poor baby," Heathcliff cried. "The victim of income tax! Just because he wears a hearing aid…"

"…and needs a shave…" put in Belladonna, running her finger critically across the baby's cheek.

"…and needs a shave," agreed Heathcliff, "you want me to throw him out into the hurricane. I'm sorry to say this, Belladonna, but too much science has made you hard-hearted."

66

"Too much magic has made you soft-headed," cried Belladonna. "That baby looks just like one of the Shoddys to me."

"This poor baby stays!" shouted Heathcliff.

"All right," said Belladonna, "but don't expect me to change his diapers."

There was a wail from inside the baby carriage.

"Look!" cried Heathcliff. "See how he clutches his diapers around him. He certainly doesn't want you to touch him, you—you—you scientist."

The children and the cats were appalled to find Heathcliff and Belladonna fighting already.

"We need music," muttered Zanzibar. Joanna ran to the school piano, Leo picked up the guitar, and together they struck up a splendidly fiery Spanish dance. Huxley, Zaza, Mary, and Maurice sang enthusiastically.

"Listen," cried Tango to Zanzibar. "They're playing my tune." Both cats began to dance so poetically that Heathcliff and Belladonna forgot their quarreling, and watched and applauded. Heathcliff's attack of unreasonable jealousy was calmed although it did not totally disappear.

"Sorry," he said.

"I'm sorry too," Belladonna answered. "Perhaps I was a little hard-hearted about the baby. He may have a heart of gold."

At that moment a loud snoring arose from the baby carriage.

"He's asleep," said Maurice.

"We'll wake him if he disturbs us when we try to work in the classroom," Heathcliff said. "It's a good chance for us to have a cup of tea while we make a few plans to fool the school inspectors. Leave the baby here to recover from the shock of his journey."

He peered into the baby carriage again. "He certainly is an odd-looking baby," he muttered, and then added quickly, "It must have been hard for his father to part with him."

"Rubbish!" said Belladonna, but she whispered it to herself so that nobody heard her.

17 · More Villainy

It was a pity they left the strange baby quite so soon, for a moment later his hearing aid began wailing eerily, and then, very faintly, a tiny crackling voice made itself heard.

"Calling Amadeus Shoddy," it said. "This is Sir Quincey Judd-Sprockett on the hearing-aid radio. Are you receiving me? Over."

Amadeus (for of course the baby was none other than he) sat bolt upright in his carriage.

"Yes!" he cried.

"Are you alone?" asked Sir Quincey.

"Yes," said Amadeus, looking around nervously.

"Listen carefully," said Sir Quincey. "Get out of your carriage..."

Amadeus stood up, and the carriage fell over with a crash.

"I am out!" he moaned, rubbing his shins.

"Good! Go to the window and open it."

"Open the window?" cried Amadeus. "You're asking an old man wearing a diaper to open the window? What about the hurricane?"

"It's on the other side of the mountain at present," said Sir Quincey impatiently. "Hurry up or it'll be back again."

Grumbling resentfully, Amadeus tottered to the window, which was set in a deep recess. It was hard to shift but at last he prized it open an inch. Immediately a grubby hand as hairy as a bear's paw and garnished around the edges with black fingernails pushed its way in. Amadeus forced the window wider, and Voltaire squeezed into the room.

"Oh, I've been having a treadful dime," he said. "It's all very well for you, wrapped up in a corm warriage, but I've been stuck out there in that Judd-Vannet camper sprock with Sir Quincey and his adapted anty, and she twirted me squice with her oil can."

"But you don't have to wear diapers and be patted by magicians and criticized by mad scientists," retorted Amadeus.

"Stop it, both of you," said Sir Quincey over the hearing-aid radio. "Where is she?"

Voltaire and Amadeus stared around blankly.

"Where's who?" whispered Amadeus.

"Dopperbella Donnler!" Voltaire whispered back. "Remember, we're stere to heal her for Sir Quincey."

"She's around somewhere," said Amadeus. "I could hear her voice insulting me, but I couldn't see her, because Sir Quincey took my glasses."

They began searching cupboards, knocking things over as they went, and hushing each other loudly. White rabbits leaped out of some of the cupboards and

flocks of doves flew out of the others. One drawer
exploded into a great bouquet of brilliant flowers.
Voltaire thought he had found a secret cubby in
Heathcliff's desk, but all it held was a hundred and
fifteen silk handkerchiefs, knotted together. There was
plenty of mystery and magic around, but no sign of
Belladonna.

Suddenly, Voltaire froze.

"Someone's coming," he cried. "Hide!"

In a moment he had sprung up beside the statue of Mrs. Desirée Thoroughgood and had twisted himself around her, striking the same heroic pose. Amadeus moved rather more slowly. He hoisted himself up on the plinth, and, crawling in under the raincoats that partially covered her, he flung his arms around her legs in intimate fashion and clung there desperately, trying not to breathe too noticeably.

The door opened and in came Tango and Zanzibar, their tails lovingly entwined.

"May I say you are the most fascinating cat I have ever met," mewed Tango.

"Thank you and likewise," purred Zanzibar.

"What a pity Heathcliff and Belladonna don't get on better," Tango said. "Then we could all go out between hurricanes and wander among the beautiful pigweed flowers."

"Oh, but the pigweed never ever flowers until the first day of spring and that's not until tomorrow," cried Zanzibar. "Pigweed flowers always open on the exact stroke of midnight."

"It's a long time to wait," said Tango.

Both cats sighed deeply. Then Zanzibar cheered up. "Never mind!" she said. "I will let you into a secret, Tango . . . a secret no one but you would understand. Every so often I sneak in here on my own, and sharpen my claws on the statue of Mrs. Desirée Thoroughgood. I don't mean any disrespect, but being carved of corkwood, she makes a very good claw-sharpener. Of course, I don't let Mr. Warlock know. Let's sharpen our claws together, shall we?"

Both cats proceeded to sharpen their claws, quite unaware that they were sharpening them on two luckless villains. Agony though it was, the Shoddys were obliged to keep completely still.

Zanzibar sighed again. "Ah, Tango, let us go up to the very tip-top of the peak, before the hurricane comes back, and try to work out a way of bringing science and magic together in wonderful harmony. I'm sure it can be done."

"A good idea!" purred Tango. "You are as clever as you are beautiful."

"Yes," agreed Zanzibar, who, like most cats, had no false modesty.

The cats left the room, and the Shoddys, father and

son, leaped down from the statue, moaning and rubbing the places where the cats had sharpened their claws. Amadeus, since he was not as hairy as Voltaire and was wearing only a diaper, looked a pathetic sight.

"Voltaire, Amadeus!" called Sir Quincey over the hearing-aid radio. "What's going on there?"

But there was a step in the hall.

"Some *else* is coming," hissed Voltaire. "Quick, into the coom brupboard." Sir Quincey sent a wicked laugh over the hearing-aid radio, just to encourage them. It echoed a little in the broom cupboard, and Heathcliff, who was just closing the classroom door, paused and looked into the air. Must be possums, he thought. Possums can laugh very wickedly when they feel like it.

He wandered around the classroom in a restless fashion, touching the clock, the blackboard, and the statue as if they were all utterly new to him. He saw Belladonna's cloak hanging from the extended arm of Mrs. Desirée Thoroughgood.

"Her cloak!" he sighed. Twitching it free, he draped it around himself. "It is as if she had her arms around me," he murmured in a sentimental voice, pacing up and down the room. "How can I—a noted sorcerer— love a scientist?" he asked the blackboard, but it couldn't—or wouldn't—tell him. "It's a doomed love!" he muttered to the clock, which sighed and scratched itself at about a quarter to ten. "I, who have devoted my life to magic, how can I dream of a girl who has devoted her life to bullying nature and inventing unnatural machines. But I love her. I love her!"

At this moment the Shoddys opened the broom-cupboard door a crack and looked out. Of course, Amadeus had not heard a word, and even Voltaire wasn't too sure what was going on. All they saw was a figure draped in Belladonna's cloak, with a mop of red hair and sticking-out ears.

"It's her!" mouthed Voltaire, pointing and making signs.

"It's her!" Amadeus said, making signs and pointing.

Voltaire grabbed the string of colored scarves he had discovered only five minutes earlier. He took one end and passed the other to Amadeus.

"A man needs more in his life than sorcery and a school on Hurricane Peak," mused Heathcliff, staring at the statue of Mrs. Thoroughgood, which had often inspired him in the past.

Amadeus and Voltaire agreed.

"A man needs money," Amadeus whispered.

"A tanner for you and a tenner for me" cried Voltaire, giving the old Shoddy war cry of *"Charge!"*

There was a sudden uproar. The clock struck ten for the second time that morning. The statue of Mrs. Thoroughgood toppled over with a resounding crash and (being made of corkwood) bounced up and down a few times. Outside in the camper van, crouched over the Judd-Sprockett control panel, Sir Quincey, listening as well as he could to what was going on, gave a wicked laugh. But the uproar could not stop

Voltaire and Amadeus taking Heathcliff by surprise. They gagged him with a silk scarf, rolled him into a sort of scientific sausage in Belladonna's cloak, and then tied him in every direction with a hundred and fifteen silk scarves, and all before he could cast a single spell. He could move neither hand nor foot. Of course, even a good magician can be slowed down by love, and for a moment Heathcliff thought this sudden attack was one of the side effects of passion, and, by the time he realized it was only two contemptible villains, it was already too late. The world whirled about him, and he fainted away, as kidnapped people who also happen to be in love often do.

What with the striking clock and the falling statue and Voltaire shouting back-to-front instructions to his father and the thumping noise of Heathcliff's struggles, everyone in the Unexpected School could tell something was going on.

Down from the tip-top of the peak rushed Tango and Zanzibar. In from the kitchen rushed the children and Belladonna, refreshments in their hands.

But by then the Shoddys had hoisted Heathcliff out of the window and were racing away with him in the direction of the Judd-Sprockett camper van. The open window flapped mockingly and the empty baby carriage told its own story.

"Heathcliff's gone!" cried Belladonna. "The man I adore—even if he is a magician. And where is that baby?"

No one could tell her. Like Heathcliff, the baby had quite vanished away.

18 · Another Wicked Laugh

Voltaire and Amadeus, with Heathcliff swinging between them, pelted toward the camper van, anxious to get there before the hurricane came back again.

"Sir Sprincey Quud-Jockett will pay us richly for this," cried Voltaire buoyantly.

But Amadeus said nothing. He was out of breath, and his diaper kept falling down. He was finding it very hard to clutch the feet of the kidnapped magician and keep up with Voltaire.

From inside the camper van Sir Quincey, looking up the path with the Judd-Sprockett "Stickybeak" periscope, laughed with glee. A moment later the sound of wicked chuckles filled the air of Hurricane Peak . . . laughter so loud that in the classroom of the Unexpected School, children, cats, and Belladonna looked up, startled.

"How wicked the possums sound," muttered Belladonna. "But I mustn't let myself be distracted by possums. We must make plans to find Heathcliff at once."

19 · Plans to Find Heathcliff

"Poor darling Heathcliff has been kidnapped by the Shoddys," cried Belladonna. "It's all my fault, for they followed me here from Hookywalker."

"Don't worry," said Maurice. "He can look after himself."

"He can bring things out of his imagination and make them seem real," cried Mary.

"He has a whole world in there," added Joanna, tapping her own head to show where Heathcliff kept his imagination. "It's like a useful cupboard. He can reach through and get a grip on anything in the world."

"He hides things in it, and then takes them out again when he needs them," added Mary.

"Mind you, they never come out quite the same as when he put them in," Zanzibar mewed.

But Belladonna was not to be comforted. She sank down at the corkwood feet of Mrs. Thoroughgood and buried her face in her hands.

The children were impressed by her despair.

"Are you terribly sad?" asked Joanna.

"Are you really in love with Mr. Warlock?" asked Zaza, frowning. Huxley said nothing, but took a few quick notes.

Belladonna sat up, looking anxious. She felt her own forehead and took her own pulse. She was certainly rather feverish.

"I might have a slight attack of love," she said. "But let's not stand around talking about it. We must find Heathcliff at once."

The children cheered vigorously.

"We'll take the front half of the peak," said Tango.

"We'll take the back half," cried Zanzibar.

Quickly they chose teams, chanting the following mystic verse:

> Icker acker water cracker,
> Icker Acker Ooo!
> Hurry, here's the hurricane!
> So out goes you!

Zanzibar chose Joanna, and Huxley and Maurice. Tango chose Mary, Leo, and Zaza.

Neither of them chose Belladonna, for everyone thought that, being a scientist, she would manage better on her own. Besides, secretly, they thought that being in love might make her a bit useless.

Within moments the whole school shook to the thunder of many stone boots, some rushing to the front door and rolling the boulder away and some blundering out the back.

"Hey!" cried Belladonna, but she was left entirely on her own.

"Why do they bother with stone boots when I could invent magnetic boots for them? Hurricane Peak is so full of iron ore that magnetic boots would be very efficient and much quieter, too." She muttered a few important scientific equations such as "$E = MC^2$" and "$e = cv$," but they did not comfort her very much.

"I feel so useless," she mumbled. "Shall I go out and search, too?" Suddenly noticing Heathcliff's cloak, she picked it up, looking at it fondly and trying to decipher the magic words embroidered on it. Then she slipped it over her shoulders. "It's as if he had his arms around me," she murmured. "Perhaps there is something, not much maybe, but *something*, in magic after all. I'll go and look for Heathcliff myself, and I'll take my little inventor's pack with me."

As soon as he saw the Shoddys plunging down the slope toward him, carrying a figure wrapped around in silk scarves, Sir Quincey Judd-Sprocket sat back in his wheelchair and sighed. He should have been very happy, for his evil schemes seemed to be working out. Yet, curiously enough, he felt a little melancholy. Like many wicked industrialists, he wanted to have all the advantages of wickedness and *still* get all the credit for being a good person, so in the very moments when things were going well, he often felt fretful and torn in two.

"I was driven to it," he muttered. "Income tax is so very high this year. And I had no parents to teach me the difference between right and wrong."

"Never mind!" said his adopted aunt, patting the top of his head. "A wicked industrialist is like a peppercorn... gives a bit of bite to the soup of life. That's what I used to say when I was a... well, whatever it was that I was before I was an adopted aunt. Look on yourself as one of society's peppercorns."

Sir Quincey cheered up at once, for he was extremely fond of pepper. At that very moment the Shoddys, father and son, carried their burden through the door.

"Quackly! Cart the stamper van!" shouted Voltaire. Aunt Perdita shot obediently to the controls, though she was clearly rather puzzled. There was certainly something about Hurricane Peak... a teasing memory that just would not go away.

"Did you *have* to stun her?" asked Sir Quincey, looking doubtfully at the unconscious figure.

"Oh yes!" said Voltaire. "We obsoletely had to."

"She might have zapped us with some laser gun or other," gasped Amadeus. "But we was too quick for her! Arh, arh, arh!" He ended his statement with a gruesome chuckle.

Aunt Perdita tried to start the camper van.

Arh! arh! arh! it went, sounding exactly like Amadeus. It did not start.

Sir Quincey, who had unwrapped some of the red and yellow scarves from around Heathcliff's face, frowned in puzzlement.

"She seems—different from the way I remember her," he said uneasily.

"That's because we hit her on the head," croaked Amadeus. "I've often noticed how being hit on the head changes a person."

"It ages them," added Voltaire, staring very hard at Heathcliff, and looking more and more annoyed. "But that's her hair and those are her ears. You've got to admit it."

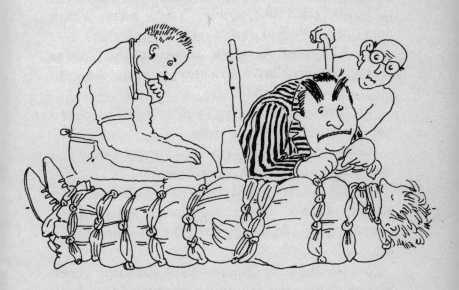

"But I wanted more than her hair and her ears!" Sir Quincey complained. "I wanted the head beneath it, the mind full of inventions between the ears. Somehow this head ..."

Arh! Argh! Argh! went the camper van, still refusing to start. Aunt Perdita tried for a third time but the

Judd-Sprockett 6-volt battery began to go flat almost at once.

"She's waking up!" cried Amadeus.

"No, she isn't," growled Sir Quincey, thinking the old villain was referring to the camper van. But Amadeus was talking about Heathcliff, who was sitting up and looking very confused.

"I can't get it going," declared Perdita. "You're all going to have to get out and push!"

"Push?" cried Sir Quincey. "You're asking a man with only one leg to push a camper van?"

"Push?" cried Amadeus incredulously. "You're asking a senior citizen with a hearing aid and diaper to push a camper van?"

"*I'm* not pushing any vamper can!" declared Voltaire, folding his hairy arms.

"Okay—don't then!" said Aunt Perdita. "We'll just stay here. I don't care. I like the view."

"Where am I?" asked Heathcliff, sitting up and staring around. "What happened? When did it happen? How did it happen? Why am I here? Who are you?"

"Madam, I am Sir Quincey Judd-Sprockett!" cried Sir Quincey, trying to sound all suave and sophisticated. "And you are Belladonna Doppler, the famous absentminded atomic scientist," he added a little more doubtfully.

"Never!" cried Heathcliff. "No way can I be a scientist. I can't tell a quark from a shark. Or a laser from a blazer," he added proudly.

"No use frying to tool us!" cried Voltaire. "Look at your hair! Look at your cloak! Look at your sticking-out ears."

Although Heathcliff's ears did stick out, they didn't stick out quite so much that he could look at them without a mirror, so he looked at his cloak, only, of course, to see it wasn't his after all.

"Madam . . . you are in my power!" cried Sir Quincey.

"Madam . . . ?" murmured Heathcliff incredulously, studying the equation $E = MC^2$ embroidered in bright red chain stitch on the cloak.

Sir Quincey tried a wicked laugh, but it collapsed into a nasty cough as usual.

"I've been stolen away by a giant possum with bronchitis," muttered Heathcliff, but he was beginning to get some idea of what had really happened to him.

". . . and now," said Sir Quincey, blushing a little, "as soon as we get the Judd-Sprockett camper van going again I will carry you off to the Judd-Sprockett laboratories so that you can invent things for me. You have power over science, and, slubberdegullion, I have power over you," he explained.

Heathcliff got to his feet.

"But suppose I don't want to go?" he asked.

"Too bad!" said Voltaire. "You've dot to goo what we say from now on."

"From now on you've got to do what *we* say," Amadeus agreed. "Too bad!"

"Suppose I plead for mercy?" asked Heathcliff slyly. "Suppose I beg you to let me go back to my humble laboratory where I can happily invent the things I want to, whether they're any good to you or not."

"Mo nursey!" declared Voltaire, or that was what it sounded like.

"None!" cried Sir Quincey, feeling he was in charge of things at last.

"Very well," cried Heathcliff. "You have stolen me away . . . that's true. But I am not without friends. Every fairy story in the world will answer the call of a true magician."

It was his turn to laugh and he laughed in a very weird manner, and without coughing once. The villains turned pale at the sound.

"That wasn't the laugh of an atomic scientist," moaned Amadeus.

"It sounds to me like a sorcerer," said Aunt Perdita critically. The villains turned even paler. It is one thing to kidnap a helpless atomic scientist, and quite another to suspect you might have kidnapped a sorcerer by mistake.

Heathcliff clenched his hands and held them high

over his head. His eyes flashed green lightning . . . his voice growled like thunder.

"I reach back into the recesses of my imagination and I bring out *darkness!*" he shouted.

Everything went black. Think, if you can, of the fathomless black bottom of the blackest ocean on the blackest night on the blackest planet in the blackest part of space. Well, everything went even blacker than that!

"Here! Where's the steering wheel gone?" cried Aunt Perdita, groping around in the dark.

"And now for the forest . . ." whispered Heathcliff, beginning to mutter in a sinister fashion.

"Mercy! mercy!" howled the Shoddys, father and son.

"There are no forests around here," blustered Sir Quincey, trying to seem brave, although his wheel-chair was rattling wildly.

"Oh, we all carry a forest in our heads," Heathcliff answered. "Red Riding Hood's wolf is always waiting for us if we stop to gather flowers. Chicken Licken cannot stop himself from meeting Mr. Fox." He took a deep breath and reached back further into his imagination. "I call on the forest!" he shouted.

It was so black you couldn't see anything and yet, all at once, the darkness began to rustle with leaves. A foresty smell came into the air. Somewhere, a wolf howled.

"Help!" shouted the Shoddys, and a thousand voices (voices of silver, voices of stone, voices of flutes

90

that were carved out of bone, voices of vampires, voices of bears, voices of wolves coming out of their lairs) all cried back, *Help!* in a ghastly, ghostly chorus.

"In the forests of magic wherever you go, you must lope like a leopard and keep your voice low!" said Heathcliff softly.

"Help!" whispered Sir Quincey. He tried to activate the rocket launcher that was concealed in the right armrest of his wheelchair, but he accidentally pressed the fast-forward button. His wheelchair, working wonderfully for once, shot off into the dark, carrying him away in it. He kicked and screamed in a cowardly fashion while the cacophonous chorus screamed along with him.

"Wait! Wait! I'm coming too," shouted Amadeus, bolting, with wonderful agility for a man of his years, into the shadows.

"Help! Holp! Hilp! Hulp!" yelled Voltaire, and, roaring like a terrified bull, he raced after them. For a moment their voices could be heard retreating in three different directions. Then they died away in silence, and the strange chorus of echoes died away too.

"How strange!" mused Heathcliff. "There is great power in this cloak. I didn't realize ... my spells have never worked so well before. Oh, Belladonna, I was wrong. You may be devoted to science and I to magic, but perhaps our powers spring from the same source after all."

"Oh, well," said Aunt Perdita, philosophically. "I

suppose this always happens when you set out to kidnap an inventor and get a magician by accident."

Light began to come back into the world...a mysterious, tender green light, and it showed trees, trees, trees—everywhere. The camper van was entirely grown over with vines that were still writhing and entwining like serpents. Hurricane Peak seemed to have vanished. Heathcliff, with Aunt Perdita beside him, stood in the biggest, oldest, wisest forest in the world.

There was a crackling sound and out from under the trees burst two figures carrying briefcases and wearing three-piece suits with respectable dove-colored ties. They skipped across the glade like agile gazelles and vanished into the greenery on the other side.

"Who were they?" asked Heathcliff. He was really taken aback himself.

"They looked like school inspectors to me!" replied Aunt Perdita, coming forward and wiping her hands on a piece of rag as she spoke.

"School inspectors!" shouted Heathcliff. "Oh dear! My poor school! My poor children! I know how to get into this wood but I'm not sure how to get myself out again."

And off he ran, Belladonna's cloak billowing out behind him.

"Just as well we motor mechanics learn to take the rough with the smooth," said Aunt Perdita, staring after him. She whistled shrilly on her fingers. "Time for a tea break," she said to herself. Fortunately she always took her giant thermos flask and a packet of biscuits with her and they, at least, had not vanished under the vines along with the rest of the camper van. She made a nice place for herself among the ferns, and settled down for a refreshing cup of tea. Suddenly she sat up straight, frowning to herself.

"But how did I know they were school inspectors?" she asked aloud. "How?"

How? the forest asked back, speaking with its many voices of animals and trees, precious metals and bones. But it didn't seem to know the answer, either.

21 · A Short Chapter

The two school inspectors jogged through the forest. They had known it would be difficult to get to the Unexpected School, but they hadn't realized it would be quite as difficult as this. One of them, Magnus Bruin, was a senior inspector who had inspected schools and teachers in Hookywalker for years and years. But he had always put off going to Hurricane Peak because of the hurricane. In fact, other inspectors began calling it the Uninspected School and nudged each other whenever it was mentioned.

The other inspector, George Tanglefoot, was just learning to be an inspector. He considered himself fortunate to be setting off with Magnus Bruin, a man of the world who would show him how to inspect properly. However, as he jogged through the forest with his briefcase bouncing painfully against one leg, he was not so sure. Going up ladders and under waterfalls, and over wibbly-wobbly bridges, lying flat on his stomach as the hurricane went past, all seemed too much to put up with. Now, he was jogging

through a forest which had suddenly appeared and was not even marked on the map.

I didn't do a degree in science and mathematics to spend my time running through forests, he thought to himself. When does the inspecting begin?

"Shall we have another look at the map?" asked Magnus Bruin at last.

The map was a very large one, as tall as one school inspector standing on another one's shoulders, and twice as wide. As they struggled to open it, a fierce gust of wind—possibly a gust that had somehow been separated from the hurricane—tore the map from their hands. It didn't much matter, for they couldn't make sense of it anyway, but they hated to lose government property, having had to sign for it. Now, they were in a forest full of echoes without a map. But they were not school inspectors for nothing.

"Advance," shouted Magnus Bruin, waving his briefcase bravely.

"Advance," agreed Tanglefoot, waving his briefcase, too.

Fat chance! the echoes said (or seemed to say) from the depths of the enchanted wood.

22 · Lost in the Forest

Zanzibar, along with Joanna, Maurice, and Huxley, had run out of the front door of the school. They had gone no distance at all when the air around them gave a curious shiver and a great forest suddenly appeared. It was not a question of hesitating on the edge of the forest and then adventuring into it. They were right in the middle of it from the very beginning, and the funny thing was that, though none of them had ever been in a forest before, they all had the feeling that they recognized it. Great, towering trunks leaped upward in every direction. Branches interlaced as if the trees were holding hands. A path opened before them, so of course they took it, for they all had the feeling that if they tried to go some other way the trees would quickly cluster together to stop them, and not one of them wanted that.

Meanwhile, Tango, along with Mary, Zaza, and Leo, had run out of the back door of the school. But scarcely had they gone a step before there was a sound as if the very rocks had sighed under them. Huge trees suddenly flowed out of the very air. It was as if the forest had been there all the time, but had only just decided to show itself, and the strange thing was this—none of them, either, had ever seen the forest before, and yet they, too, all seemed to recognize it.

"It's magic!" said Maurice. "I get pins and needles whenever someone is using magic, and I've got pins and needles in my feet now."

"Magic!" said Tango. "That probably means Mr. Warlock is somewhere close at hand. Mr. Warlock!" he mewed loudly, and to his amazement a thousand voices answered him. There were hooting voices, howling voices, laughing voices, wailing voices,

mewing voices, barking voices, young voices, old voices, tin voices, gold voices, and they all said *Mr. Warlock, Mr. Warlock!* over and over again.

"Echoes!" cried Mary.

"Ghosts!" cried Leo.

"I think it's the elements," said Tango.

"The elephants?" asked Leo hopefully. He would have enjoyed seeing a few elephants.

"The elements!" Tango said. "I know all about the elements because of helping Belladonna with her inventions. I think it's the natural elements—all eighty-eight of them—talking back to us, and possibly a few man-made ones too."

"You're only guessing wildly," said Zaza.

"Well, we cats are pretty close to nature," said Tango. "I think this forest is so old that it goes back to the beginning of all things when the elements could talk. But there's no sense in wasting time speculating about that. Come on. Let's keep on searching. Advance!" he shouted, and the echo-voices shouted as well.

Off they plunged down the track. Then a strange thing happened. Once they had vanished, the trees shifted. If anyone had been standing there they would have seen them shift, though not quite *how* they shifted, for it was done in the blink of an eye. One moment the path ran one way, in the next moment it was gone, and another path was revealed. Clumping down the new path in their stone boots came the other half of the Unexpected School.

"Mr. Warlock!" shouted Zanzibar.

Mr. Warlock, the voices shouted back.

"What wonderful echoes!" Maurice said, pausing. Huxley agreed. *The echoes in the enchanted wood make a sort of musical thunder,* he scribbled quickly in his notebook.

"I think it is magical spirits," Zanzibar mewed. "I think in this forest everything has a voice and can answer us. If only we had time to listen we would hear them all. But we must find poor Mr. Warlock at once. Remember, the school inspectors will be here today, and what will they think when they find the school empty and nobody doing any science or math. They'll close the school and sell the land to Sir Quincey Judd-Sprockett."

Off they all ran down the path, but no sooner had they vanished than the forest gave a deep mysterious sigh and changed again. Down a third path came Belladonna, wearing Heathcliff's cloak around her shoulders.

"How very strange!" she said, pausing and touching the tree trunks curiously. "This forest is wonderful but it is not quite real. Almost real, but not quite real enough to fool a scientist. What does it mean? Can it be that besides photons and protons, neutrinos and quarks, there really are forests of echoes and snarks? Then magic might turn out to be important after all."

She pulled Heathcliff's cloak more snugly around her and wandered off down the path. The trees silently closed behind her and made way for Heathcliff himself, anxiously searching for a way out of the forest. Having brought it out of his imagination he found, now, it was too big to fit it back again.

"I must get home before the inspectors arrive," he muttered, vanishing among the shifting trees.

Along an entirely different path came Amadeus and Voltaire, pulling Sir Quincey's wheelchair, with Sir Quincey himself sitting in it, looking very bad-tempered.

"Faster, faster!" he was shouting. "We must get out of here."

"You should be ashamed ... making a senior citizen pull a wheelchair," Amadeus cried.

"You should be ashamed bringing me a sorcerer instead of a scientist," Sir Quincey yelled back.

"That was definitely Belladonna Doppler," cried Amadeus. "She must have been taking magic lessons in her spare time."

"This way!" said Voltaire, moving down the only path he could see. Immediately, the forest swallowed them, but no sooner had they gone than the two school inspectors came jogging out of the shadows once more.

"Where are we?" cried Mr. Bruin, collapsing against a tree, utterly exhausted.

"On Hurricane Peak, sir!" explained Tanglefoot quickly.

"But whereabouts on Hurricane Peak, and when

and why and how?" cried Bruin. "And what's happened to the hurricane? It's late." He sounded very cross with the hurricane for being late.

"Sir," said Tanglefoot earnestly, "I'd like to point out how suddenly this forest appeared. One moment no forest . . . the next moment forest everywhere. Looks like magic to me!"

"I'm sorry to hear someone who has risen to be a school inspector talking about magic," said Bruin. "There is no such thing, Tanglefoot. This forest must be something to do with science, but I don't know what. Now, follow me!"

And he led Tanglefoot firmly down a path and disappeared. The path changed again.

Aunt Perdita appeared with her thermos flask and packet of biscuits. Suddenly, from between the trees like a flapping, crackling ghost, a map of Hurricane Peak blew wildly toward her. She snatched it out of the air and began to fold it up with no trouble at all. That was the sort of aunt she was. While she did this, the trees flicked into a new pattern, and out of the soft shadows came Tango and his group of children, going in the opposite direction from the one in which he had started off. It was all very confusing.

23 · Echoes

"Mr. Warlock!" called Tango, but not very loudly. He was exhausted. He flopped down under a tree and began to lick his paws.

"It's very strange," began Leo. "I can feel Mr. Warlock all around me and yet there isn't a sign of him anywhere."

"He must have heard us calling him," Mary declared. "What with the echoes," she added. "Hello!" she shouted.

The voices all called *Hello!* back to her, but this time Mary thought she detected some other ordinary voices mixed in with them—voices she knew.

"Hello!" she called again.

Hello! the voices called back. Some of them sounded closer.

Even Tango forgot his tired paws and sat up alertly.

"I hear the mewing of the one I love," he said. "Hello!" he caterwauled. *Hello* the echoes called back. There was a distinct caterwauling sound among them.

A moment later Zanzibar burst out of the forest,

followed by Joanna, Maurice, and Huxley.

"Oh, it's you!" Zanzibar cried. "We thought we had found Mr. Warlock."

"Oh, it's you," said Tango. "Were you that echo all the time?"

"I'm not sure," said Zanzibar. "'The wood is full of noises, sounds and sweet airs that give a delight and hurt not. Sometimes a thousand twangling instruments will hum about my ears and sometimes voices ...'"

"That's very good," cried Tango, full of admiration. As he had been brought up on science and math, he did not recognize that Zanzibar was quoting Shakespeare. "You've certainly got a way with words."

"I've got away with those ones, anyway," Zanzibar replied. "Perhaps we have been chasing one another all this time. Why didn't you keep to the path?"

"Why didn't *you* keep to it?" Tango asked back.

"We did," Zanzibar declared.

"We haven't been off the path once," said Huxley.

"But neither have we," said Leo. "Look, it's over there."

But it wasn't!

"*There* it is," said Zaza triumphantly. Everyone looked to where she pointed, but there was no path there, either. Huxley scratched his head. Tango scratched his ear.

"There is something very strange about this forest," said Zanzibar. "Look. There's only one path and it's over there, but we certainly didn't come that way."

They all stared hard at the path, but it didn't move an inch.

"Well, we'd better go that way," Tango said. "But let's all stick together this time."

"Yes, let's," said Maurice.

"If you squinch your eyes up and look at this forest sideways it looks like a mouthful of very big teeth," said Zaza. "It might swallow us up!" She wished she had her felt-tip pens with her so that she could make a quick sketch.

"What nonsense," said Zanzibar very briskly. "Stop that blood-and-thunder talk and follow me."

"Follow me, too," said Tango, hurrying to Zanzibar's side. The two cats curled their tails together and set off up the path, the children following.

It really was a very mysterious forest. Once, far away among the shadows and the giant ferns and mosses, Joanna thought she glimpsed a little house made out of barley sugar, gingerbread, and chocolate, but there was no time to investigate. The path turned a corner and she did not see it again. Maurice, looking between the trees, saw a girl with a red hood walking beside a wolf, while Leo thought he saw sly Foxy Loxy slinking by with Chicken Licken, Goosey Loosey, and Turkey Lurkey, all glancing up at the invisible sky as if they thought it might be falling. Zaza believed she saw three bears wandering along in the dim foresty distance, but just as she was about to point them out Tango cried, "There, ahead of us! Mr. Warlock!"

"I distinctly saw his cloak!" said Zanzibar. "Hurry!"

"Are you there?" called a voice.

"Here we are!" everyone called back, and Zanzibar added, "Just wait where you are and we'll catch up with you!" The path wound around a corner and into a little glade full of soft green mosses and enormous, curling vines. When the children and cats burst into the glade they found someone waiting there for them.

Two men in suits and ties, carrying briefcases, were already standing there, looking very out of place in that wild story-book forest. Against the great tangle of vines someone had made a neat little tent out of a huge government map, but the children had no time to think about that. The men were staring at them at first in surprise and then later in a particularly suspicious fashion.

"I'm so sorry," said Zanzibar in very ladylike tones. "We were looking for Mr. Warlock!"

"But we were looking for him, too," said the short, fat man with the dove-colored tie. "May I ask who you are?"

"We are pupils of the Unexpected School," Zanzibar said haughtily, "and I am the head prefect."

"I thought so!" cried the man triumphantly. "Take a note, Tanglefoot. The Unexpected School was wandering around in the forest instead of being in the classroom concentrating on science and math and waiting to be inspected."

"We can begin the inspection at once," cried Tanglefoot happily.

"Oh, miaow!" cried Zanzibar.

The children were silent with horror. They thought of running away, but they knew that running away from school inspectors would mean bad marks for their school, and besides, if they went off the track there might be foxes and wolves and bears waiting to snap them up.

"Make a note that they are wandering in the woods with no teacher to keep an eye on them, and only a cat for head prefect," said Magnus Bruin in a lordly voice. "Poor little things," he added less convincingly.

"I beg your pardon," said a voice, "but they are not poor little things. Zanzibar is a very good head prefect and I am here to keep an eye on them."

Everyone turned. Out of the forest appeared a figure in a cloak inscribed with equations such as $E = MC^2$ and $e = cv$ and other scientific and mathematical data. Wearing Belladonna's cloak,

Heathcliff looked the very picture of a good teacher of science and math, and for a moment Magnus Bruin was convinced.

"But what are you doing wandering here in the wood, when you should be teaching in school?" he asked cunningly.

"A good question," Heathcliff replied, thinking quickly. "We are on a nature ramble."

"A nature ramble!" muttered Tanglefoot, writing it all down.

"Well, now," said Magnus Bruin, looking down at the children, "and what have you learned this morning?"

"This evening," said Tanglefoot quickly.

"Morning, Tanglefoot! It must be morning by now."

"I *think* it's midafternoon," said Heathcliff.

But none of them was sure of time anymore. Tanglefoot, Magnus Bruin, and Huxley all looked at their watches and found it was five to twelve. Even Huxley's luminous technicolor cuckooing watch, which showed the year as well as the time of day, told you when there was going to be a total eclipse of the sun or the moon, and mentioned the date when Halley's Comet would return, and a lot of useful things of that sort, merely said five to twelve. But whether it was day or night was impossible to work out. There seemed to be no day and no night under the leaves of that particular forest.

"Anyhow," said Magnus Bruin, looking at Heathcliff very suspiciously, "you can call this a nature walk if you like, but I think you are lost in the woods like the rest of us."

"No such thing," said Heathcliff airily, although, having summoned this enchanted wood out of nowhere, he really didn't have the least idea how to get out of it.

"Then take us back to the school and give us a weak cup of tea and a biscuit," begged Magnus Bruin, "because Tanglefoot and I are worn out with wandering on Hurricane Peak."

But they were interrupted. The tent behind them crackled slightly, and a woman in blue overalls crawled out of it.

"Would you believe it?" she said. "No gas. That's all that's wrong with it. The gas gauge was giving a faulty reading. Of course, it's a Judd-Sprockett gas gauge so what more could you expect? But where am I going to get any gas in this forest? Someone will have to walk down to Hookywalker and buy some. That's all."

Everyone stared at her, but nobody offered to go.

"Did someone ask about a cup of tea?" she went on. "I have plenty left in my giant thermos."

"Just a moment," said Heathcliff, staring at her intently. "Haven't we met before?"

"I don't think so," she said, looking surprised.

"Yet I know your face," Heathcliff cried, and all the children from the school looked at her with the same puzzled expression. They all felt they knew her, but didn't know how they could, for they had certainly never seen her before.

"Come into the tent and talk it over," she said. "There's plenty of room. It's made out of a very big government map I found blowing through the forest after my adopted nephew ran off and left me ... not that he'll get far. His wheelchair will be breaking down at any moment now. It's a Judd-Sprockett invention."

"No," said Heathcliff. "I've got to take the inspectors back to the school. And besides, I have to tell Belladonna I love her madly even if she is a scientist."

"Just a moment," cried a dread voice. "No one is going anywhere to tell anyone anything unless *I* say so."

Out of the woods burst Sir Quincey Judd-Sprockett, drawn by his two vile minions, the terrible Shoddys—father and son. Sir Quincey held a gun in his right hand. "I have here a tranquilizing

gun," he announced, "and unless she comes quietly—
no more tricks, no more trees!—I'm going to
tranquilize Belladonna Doppler and carry her off to
my house on the shady side of Hookywalker."

He was looking at Heathcliff, of course.

24 · The Pigweed Blossoms

All the children began shouting at once.

"It's not Belladonna Doppler, it's Heathcliff Warlock!" and the Shoddys shouted, "It *is* Bolladinner Deppler! Look at her cloak. Look at her ears!"

Magnus Bruin turned to Heathcliff very sternly.

"You told me you were Heathcliff Warlock, the headmaster of this school," he said, "and now it turns out you are Belladonna Doppler, the inventor. It won't look good on the report."

"In my hand I have a loaded tranquilizing gun . . ." began Sir Quincey sternly, but everyone was arguing too loudly to take any notice. Sir Quincey tried again.

"In my hand I am holding a loaded tranquilizing gun . . ."

"You're holding it the wrong way round, Quince!" hissed Aunt Perdita. ("Quince!" she muttered to herself. "Why am I calling him Quince all of a sudden?")

"In my hand . . ." began Sir Quincey, hastily turning the gun round the right way.

"I tell you I *am* Heathcliff Warlock," Heathcliff was

saying, but Magnus Bruin didn't believe him.

"If a famous, wicked industrialist says you are Belladonna Doppler," he said, "that's good enough for me."

"The cloak's right, the hair's right, and the ears are right," whispered Amadeus uneasily to Voltaire, "but the face is all wrong."

"Look," Voltaire whispered back. "We don't care if it is Doppabella Donnler or Warcliff Heathlock . . . as long as we get paid and get home—in that order or the other way round."

"Confess!" said Magnus Bruin, pushing in front of Sir Quincey to confront Heathcliff. "You *are* Belladonna Doppler, the famous, mad scientist."

"You are speaking of the scientist I love," cried Heathcliff. "I am merely wearing her cloak, that's all."

"Her cloak!" exclaimed Sir Quincey. "Let me get to the bottom of this." His Aunt Perdita was staring at him as if she were seeing him for the first time in years.

"Bottom? Quince?" she muttered to herself as if she were not too sure. "It's Bottomley Quince!"

"When I wear her cloak it is as if she had her arms around me," explained Heathcliff, which made Amadeus growl with disgust and Voltaire pretend to be sick.

"Oh, Heathcliff! Is that true?" cried a voice.

Everyone turned, and out of the forest came Belladonna herself, wearing Heathcliff's cloak.

"Yes," said Heathcliff. "I have fought against it. The

last thing I want to do is fall in love with a scientist, but the feeling is too strong. Belladonna, I love you."

"I love you too," Belladonna replied, causing Amadeus and Voltaire more revulsion, though the children cheered and the cats twined their tails into the shape of a heart.

"Well, at last I know who to tranquilize," shouted Sir Quincey and he pointed the gun at Belladonna (who was taking no notice of him at all). He pressed the trigger and the gun exploded—not with a dart, but with a big bunch of wonderful flowers of the kind magicians bring out of hats, and a little flag with the word BANG on it. Everyone laughed. Sir Quincey turned white with rage. He hated being laughed at.

"Very well," he cried. "If you won't *choose* to recognize the power of a wicked industrialist, you shall all be *forced* to recognize the power of a wicked industrialist. I shall blow up this whole glade with my rocket launcher . . . and everyone, except me and my minions, will be blown up along with it. That will show you."

As his hand hovered over the button, however, a tiny sound made itself heard. It was almost like the first cuckoo of spring, and yet it wasn't quite. It was Huxley's watch chiming midnight and, as the last stroke died away, the whole glade was suddenly transformed. Between the trees and on the vines covering the camper van, great flowers like golden lilies opened and filled the air with a wonderful scent. Immediately, Sir Quincey sneezed, and then he sneezed again. He sneezed a third time, and then began sneezing so quickly that it was like a rapid bombardment.

At that very moment, his aunt, who had been looking so bewildered only a moment ago, straightened up with a new light in her eye.

"What is going on here?" she demanded in a voice so brisk and barking that Tango and Zanzibar puffed their tails up as if they had heard a dog. "Bottomley Quince! You wicked boy! Take your hand off that rocket launcher. Write out five thousand times: *I must not launch rockets at school inspectors and cats!*"

At the sound of this new voice everyone turned. Everyone gasped ... everyone except Sir Quincey, who was convulsed with terrible sneezes. The delicate pollen of the pigweed blossom had brought on an overwhelming attack of hay fever.

Aunt Perdita had changed. There was no doubt about it. Mrs. Desirée Thoroughgood stood once again upon Hurricane Peak.

Heathcliff's enchantment must have been wearing

a little thin by that stage. The magical forest quivered slightly under the impact of Sir Quincey's sneezes.

"Oh, dear, it's starting to fade," Heathcliff said. "We'd better get out of here before we begin to fade with it."

Sir Quincey sneezed again. There was quite a gale. Everyone thought that it was all Sir Quincey's doing, for it took them a moment to realize that, what with the forest fading and the noisy sneezes, the hurricane had found out where they were. In another moment, yellow with the pollen of pigweed, the hurricane was upon them.

25 · Almost the End

"We must get out of here!" called Heathcliff. "We don't want to fade. And we don't want to be blown away."

"Into the camper van," shouted Amadeus in a cowardly way. He tried to bolt into it ahead of everyone else, but Voltaire seized him and flung him to the back of the line.

"It needs gas," Mrs. Thoroughgood warned them. "It won't go without it."

"How lucky I brought my little inventor's pack," said Belladonna. "I think . . ." she scrummaged in the pack. "Yes, I have brought my new concentrated dehydrated emergency gasoline pill."

The forest around her sighed and wavered like the reflection of a forest seen on a lake at evening. The air began to sigh and then to roar. The world began to flicker past like a video on fast forward.

"Quickly!" moaned Amadeus. "Oh, if we get out of this I will send Voltaire back to school and make sure he does his homework, and I'll take away his earplugs so that he learns to put words the right way round."

Belladonna brought out a large yellow pill.

"The concentrated dehydrated emergency gasoline pill," she said, holding it up for all to see. "But we need water to add to it."

"My thermos!" cried Mrs. Thoroughgood. The vines on the camper van were withering from the buffeting by the hurricane. The wheelchair rocked on its big tires, and Sir Quincey was flung violently against his own cocktail cabinet, causing his nose to bleed. He sneezed again and the whole control panel was spattered with scarlet. Meanwhile, Belladonna, having located the gasoline cap, dropped the pill into the gas tank of the camper van, and Mrs. Thoroughgood upended the thermos after it. She had drunk quite a lot of tea but there was still plenty left to allow the concentrated dehydrated emergency gasoline pill to begin working.

"It'll have to do," Belladonna said. "If only we can get out of this forest and back to the school!"

Mrs. Thoroughgood leaped into the driver's seat.

"Now, let's see!" she said, in such a determined tone that the camper van would hardly have dared not start, whether it had any gas or not. But its mighty engine leaped to life, and soon they were bumping along through the dissolving forest, dodging ghostly trees. Nobody in the camper van faded, however, though Heathcliff looked somewhat ghostly himself. After all, the forest had been made visible through his sorcery, so it was only to be expected that it would have an effect on him as it vanished. Belladonna put her arm around him and he immediately felt a lot better. The hurricane rocked them to and fro, but though, every so often, it blew a mountain goat or an ibex past them, the van was too heavily loaded, what with children, villains, stone shoes, thermos flasks, briefcases, and so on, for the hurricane to lift it into the air, and much too crowded for its walls to collapse.

"It took sorcery to get us into the forest," Belladonna pointed out, "but it has taken science to get us out."

And Heathcliff had to admit that that was perfectly true. Holding hands, they smiled at each other.

A moment later the forest had returned to where it had come from—back into the tangled dreams of the children and villains and school inspectors, and into all the fairy tales in all the libraries in Hookywalker, and all the drawings on all the walls of all the schools in the world.

Directly in front of them lay their own Unexpected School, and directly behind them came the rest of the hurricane, whirling dust and dead leaves into the air and looking as if it would like nothing better than to get a camper van full of people between its huge paws.

"Make a human chain," called Mrs. Thoroughgood calmly. "Those in stone boots go first."

The children set off, then came Heathcliff and Belladonna, who were still holding hands, then Amadeus, then Magnus Bruin, then Voltaire and then Tanglefoot, and finally, weighing the human chain down at the end, Mrs. Desirée Thoroughgood in all her majesty, dragging the wheelchair holding Sir Quincey, who looked very like a boy who expects to be given a telling off. And everywhere the pigweed was in flower. Even the hurricane could not blow it away.

26 · The End

"At last, safe home again," said Heathcliff, and Zanzibar began to purr. Heathcliff turned and faced the school inspectors.

"Any complaints you may have, you can take up with Mrs. Thoroughgood, who has been away at a conference," he said boldly. "I am only the deputy head. I teach magic and associated studies."

"I have much to say about the conduct of this school . . ." began Magnus Bruin in a trembling voice, though he avoided Mrs. Thoroughgood's eye. "I shall put it all down in my report."

Yet all of a sudden there was the sound of a quavering cry and then someone bonged the gong at the front door.

"The postman!" exclaimed Zanzibar. "What is he doing here at this hour in the morning?" And she ran to the door.

Meanwhile, Sir Quincey's sneezes had quieted a little and he was staring around the classroom with amazement.

"Why I—I seem to know this place," he cried.

"I seem to recollect that very statue. Is *this* the Unexpected School?"

Heathcliff had to admit it was.

"And this is the statue of Mrs. Thoroughgood," he added, picking it up from the floor and removing the raincoats. Once everyone could see it properly they cried out in astonishment, for the Mrs. Thoroughgood who had once been Aunt Perdita and the Mrs. Thoroughgood carved out of corkwood had exactly the same powerful eyes and exactly the same nose, indeed exactly the same everything.

"The very last thing I remember was rushing outside after bad Bottomley Quince," cried Mrs. Thoroughgood. "I was snatched up in the hurricane and I think I must have been struck by a goat or something. At any rate the next thing I remember was being adopted as the aunt of Sir Quincey Judd-Sprockett and doing all his mechanical repairs for him."

Sir Quincey turned pale. "I admit it," he said in a low voice. "I was Bottomley Quince. I used the money I stole from my fellow pupils to launch myself on a career of villainy. It is all so long ago, and I have been so bad, that I find the details hard to remember. All the same, yes, I kept Mrs. Thoroughgood at my side telling her she was my adopted aunt. I was afraid that if I let her wander away she might meet some former pupils who would tell her who she was and she would be after me again. I did wrong" (here he sneezed a few times), "and now look at me . . . a broken man."

"Not broken, just a bit cracked," Tango whispered to Zanzibar, who couldn't help smirking in the way cats do.

"And this . . . this is the classroom of my childhood," said Sir Quincey. "If I hadn't run out into the storm, if I hadn't been whirled away by the hurricane, and my dear teacher with me, she might have dragged me back in here by the ear, and I might have been a wiser and better man. Never mind! It is not too late. I shall donate a large sum of money—well, a fairly large sum—toward buying computers for the school. Would one each be enough?"

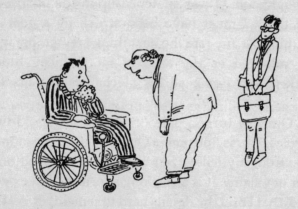

Magnus Bruin cleared his throat.

"I am sorry," he said firmly. "I am afraid this school must close down. My colleague and I are not happy with the way things are being done here. There is too much wandering about in enchanted woods and not enough science and math."

"But I am marrying an atomic scientist," cried Heathcliff. Magnus Bruin's expression changed. He had not thought of that.

"I will be happy to take the science classes in between inventing," Belladonna said.

"But what about the wandering around during school hours?" asked Tanglefoot. "It's all very well to call it a nature ramble but ..."

"Oh, that was part of a study of echoes," Belladonna said calmly.

"Echoes!" exclaimed the astonished school inspectors.

"Don't you know what echoes are?" Belladonna asked, looking surprised. "They are the repetition of sound caused by the reflection of soundwaves from something denser than air ... usually a rigid and vertical surface. You see, a secondary sound is constituted by the said reflected waves. There was a lot of that going on in the forest, or didn't you notice?"

"Darling!" exclaimed Heathcliff in a soppy voice, for he quickly saw that scientific talk like this might save the Unexpected School.

"Exactly!" said Mrs. Thoroughgood, looking pleased. She turned to the children. "Write that down!" she commanded them.

"And I will donate an underground laboratory where industrial research can take place," cried Sir Quincey. He was anxious to seem nice now, though in his heart of hearts he was already planning to steal some of Belladonna's inventions for his own companies to manufacture, and to do as much mining as possible while the underground laboratory was being installed.

"Oh, well," said Magnus Bruin in a rather grumbling voice, "if you can promise a reasonable standard of science and math perhaps we'll let you continue."

"And perhaps Voltaire and me could attend a few classes," Amadeus begged Sir Quincey in a very fawning voice. "You know, I see it all so plainly now, sir... If we had had the benefit of a good education..."

"You'll have to behave particularly well, though," said Heathcliff sternly.

"Oh, yes!" cried Amadeus, and Voltaire nodded rather sulkily.

"No more kidnapping or spying," warned Belladonna.

"Perish the thought!" cried Amadeus in a pious voice.

"We'll be podel mupils!" promised Voltaire, though Huxley, who was standing behind him, noticed he crossed his fingers as he spoke, so it wasn't a promise he was planning to keep.

"And what about me?" cried the postman. "Fighting my way up here in the early hours of the morning to deliver a special mailbag full of pink envelopes . . ."

It was most mysterious. There was a pink envelope for everyone, even for Amadeus and Voltaire, who certainly didn't deserve any letters and could not read, anyway.

"How strange!" said Belladonna. "This is an invitation to my own wedding, and yet, strictly speaking, Heathcliff hasn't accepted my offer of marriage."

"I accept it now!" said Heathcliff. "It really is a happy ending. You see what magic can achieve?"

"I think it has brought about an effect of time dilation," Belladonna said. "I think we are in tomorrow, although there are some secondary effects from yesterday. Yet time isn't a rigid surface, more of an infinitely retreating one . . ."

In the meantime, the postman was sidling up to Mrs. Thoroughgood.

"Mrs. Thoroughgood," he was saying. "I know you've only just got back, but if you could think of coming to the post office beanfeast with me..."

"The inspection is almost at an end," cried Tanglefoot, seeing that Magnus Bruin was greatly mollified by being invited to a wedding. "All that remains is to find out if the pupils are well rounded."

The children looked at each other. They hadn't realized they were going to be tested for roundness as well.

"I mean, are they good at poetry as well as science and math? Well-rounded pupils are good at both."

All the children laughed, knowing how very well rounded they truly were.

"I will want a full report on all this," said Magnus Bruin. But Heathcliff and Belladonna were holding hands, and Mrs. Thoroughgood was looking very thoughtfully at the postman, possibly thinking he might make a postmaster general with a bit of proper encouragement, and the Shoddys were polishing Sir Quincey's boot. The children were doing magic tricks or playing musical instruments, while the cats danced elegantly together. Only Huxley and Zaza were listening to the inspector.

"*I'll* write the report for you," promised Huxley. "I've given up blood-and-thunder stories and I'm going to write about real life."

"And I'll do the pictures," said Zaza.

Magnus Bruin was forced to be content with that.

And that very night Huxley began the report. He wrote on the top of his piece of paper, *The Remarkable Blood-and-Thunder Events on Hurricane Peak* (for there had been quite a lot of blood-and-thunder in real life, what with the hurricane and Sir Quincey's bleeding nose).

Huxley admired the title page of his report. He had left plenty of room for the illustrations. At last he wrote

Chapter One
A Famous Wicked Industrialist

Most stories start in one place and then go in all directions, but the strange story of the blood-and-thunder events on Hurricane Peak began in every direction and ended in one place . . .

Having gotten off to a good start, he turned to the last page and wrote the end of the report in poetry so he would know just where the report was going to.

Good luck is free to fly or flow . . .
And after all — you never know!

Then he smiled and settled down to writing everything that came between. And he was right.

You never *do* know, do you?